Things That Go Bump
in the Night

A York State Book

By Louis C. Jones

CLUBS OF THE GEORGIAN RAKES
SPOOKS OF THE VALLEY
COOPERSTOWN
MURDER AT CHERRY HILL
THREE EYES ON THE PAST

With Agnes Halsey Jones

NEW FOUND FOLK ART OF THE YOUNG REPUBLIC
QUEENA STOVALL, ARTIST OF THE BLUE RIDGE PIEDMONT

LOUIS C. JONES

Things That Go Bump in the Night

Illustrated by ERWIN AUSTIN

 SYRACUSE UNIVERSITY PRESS

Syracuse University Press Edition 1983
Syracuse, New York 13244-5160

92 93 94 95 96 97 98 99   8 7 6 5

Library of Congress Cataloging in Publication Data

Jones, Louis Clark, 1908–
    Things that go bump in the night.

    (A York State book)
    Reprint. Originally published: New York : Hill and
Wang, 1959.
    Includes index.
    1. Ghosts—United States.   I. Title.
[BF1472.U6J66   1983]   133.1'0973   83-356
ISBN 0-8156-0184-0 (pbk.)

Manufactured in the United States of America

Contents

Preface to New Edition

Naturally I welcome this new edition of *Things That Go Bump in the Night* from the friendly hands of Syracuse University Press which has become the foremost publisher of the many-faceted story of New York State. In the quarter-century since the first edition there has burgeoned a whole new interest in and acceptance of the supernatural in all its phases. This volume was not designed to persuade anyone of anything, but rather to report what the people said about the dead they believed returned. I was not, am not, a believer in the supernatural; if I had had a motto it would probably have been, *Dubito Ergo Sum*. What has long mattered to me is the pattern of oral traditions that continue to have a vigorous life of their own.

There have been some changes since the first Preface was written. We no longer live by the hang yard along the banks of the Susquehanna. We moved next door to live in Ann Cooper Pomeroy's herringbone house, and while we have never seen her, my wife thinks our old Sheltie, Fido, watched her come down the stairs and go out the front door one summer's evening. Next door the portrait of Mrs. Worthington is still bolted to the stairwell wall; the Indian is quiescent. Children in the village retell these stories and now and then add a new adventure of the restless dead—such as the schoolmaster who comes back to a house on Pine Boulevard, and others told of in the village and along the lake shore.

Harold Thompson is long gone, but his remarkable archive of folklore is housed in the New York State Historical Association library along with my own, making a total of twenty-five steel filing case drawers of the folklore current in the 30s, 40s, and 50s. Syracuse University Press has recently republished his *Body, Boots, and Britches* which remains the best collection of New York State folklore that we have.

I have made no attempt to revise or correct the text, even where I am embarassed by my own carelessness. For example, there are a number of errors of fact in the account of the ghost at Cherry Hill, but since the conclusions are correct and since I have expounded on this case elsewhere and at great length I have left it alone to keep me humble.

I've detained you long enough. Turn to the original Preface and then to the tales the people tell. A people without their own body of folklore are poverty stricken, and of this we Yorkers cannot complain.

Cooperstown, New York
31 December 1982   LCJ

Preface from an Old Hang Yard

It is a great privilege to live in a town which the dead have not deserted. Walk the streets of Cooperstown with me on a moonlight night and I'll show you a village where the enchantment of death is a warm and friendly quality. We leave my house in the old hang yard, cross the Susquehanna River at its source, and there at River Street and Main under a

mammoth pine tree stands Pomeroy Place where old Ann
Cooper Pomeroy came back long after her death to tend the
house her rich descendants seldom used. Once, a clergyman
seeking the Episcopal rectory listened to her directions without the slightest suspicion that she had been in Christ Church
yard for many a long decade, but he identified her picture
next day without any trouble.

Next door to Pomeroy Place is Greencrest where a dead
wife came back to raise Cain every time her successor took
down that huge portrait in the stairwell. Across the street on
Sheldon Keck's property there is just a slight depression in
the earth that tells where Richard Cooper's house stood. For
years after his departure the Cooper family abstained from
using his great leather chair, because Uncle Richard was sitting in it. It was from the Keck's house, Byberry Cottage, that
Susan Fenimore Cooper, the novelist's daughter, set forth in
her wheel chair a few moments after she died, crossed River
Street, wheeled into Christ Church and down the aisle during
Good Friday service, right through the altar, and disappeared. Susan had always had "power" and one could have
expected little less from her.

In that same block there is an Indian buried behind the
stone wall. Once every few years he pushes the wall out onto
the sidewalk; I noticed the other night it's beginning to bulge
again.

One reason we in Cooperstown may be luckier than most
villages is that forty years ago Judge James Fenimore Cooper,
grandson of the novelist, wrote down the stories he had heard
and his townsmen keep on repeating them with variations
and embroideries. And don't think these are the only haunts

we have. Over at Dr. Goodwin's house and up Otsego Lake at Hyde Hall the restless dead have long been said to break the peace and quiet of the night and the serenity of their latter-day tenants. At least this is what the people say happened; this is our legendry, our folklore, and all around us here in the heart of upstate New York there are similar legends.

And that's what this book is about: the stories of ghosts kept alive by the telling and retelling of our people. This is not a scientist's report on psychic phenomena, it is not a handbook for scaring children at summer camps, it is not history; it is folklore as it was found in New York State about a dozen years ago.

One of the assets of New York State is that from its very beginning people came here from all over Europe—Dutchmen, Germans, Frenchmen, Scots, Irish, Englishmen, Negroes, Portuguese Jews, and Swedes were all here by the eighteenth century, and I think this polyglottery has helped to give us a rich and varied folk tradition. These stories reflect the length and breadth of this cultural patchwork quilt. Most of the tales are of York State ghosts told by York State people, but not all, for I have chosen to include tales brought here from Europe by the latecomers, told now to very American grandchildren as part of their family "knapsack of memories." I am reasonably sure that many of the stories now deeply rooted in New York countryside first came to us in this same manner.

It was my privilege to teach from 1934 to 1946 at the New York State College for Teachers in Albany. I say "privilege" advisedly because there were some exceedingly interesting minds on the faculty and a bright, hard-working student body deriving from every cultural background you could imagine. One of my colleagues and close friend was Professor Harold W. Thompson, who gave a course in American Folklore, the first, I believe, offered to undergraduates. Students not only studied songs, stories, and beliefs of our people, they went into their own family circles and their home towns and collected their own traditions. Thompson's sending students out to discover their own personal heritage has always seemed to me inspired teaching.

I came to know something of the impact of this experience after he left Albany for Cornell in 1940. I had been interested in folklore from the time I heard Carl Sandburg sing and talk at Hamilton College in 1929, and I had had time to do a certain amount of collecting, writing, and studying, always with Harold Thompson's encouragement and support. So it was that I inherited the teaching of "Eng. 40: American Folklore" and taught it in fall, spring, and summer for the next six years. More than a thousand students and I taught each other the legendry and singing tradition of our state. This is the place to make unmistakably clear my indebtedness to them, for they spread a dragnet across New York, bringing in child lore, proverbs, songs, tall tales, short tales, legends, and especially tales of the supernatural. Thompson can sing and play the piano, he knows music thoroughly, and he stressed the musical tradition. I'm tone deaf and lung power is my only musical asset, but I had always been intrigued by ghosts and witches, the Devil and all his followers. Being smart students, they most particularly sought what interested teacher; Thompson's archive is rich in songs, mine in the supernatural. The two-hundred-odd stories in this volume are only a fifth

of the total number of ghost tales these young people garnered from kith and kin. The Archive of New York Folklore,
which contains all of their findings, now is available to scholars and students in our library at the New York State Historical Association at Cooperstown, filling two steel filing cabi-
nets to capacity. It always seems sizable until I look at the far
greater archive in Harold Thompson's office at Cornell.

As I have said, this book stems from the work of my students, and I know that neither I nor any other one person
could have made a collection of this scope. But there are dis-
advantages in having someone else do your field work. There
wasn't time to teach thoroughly the techniques of collecting,
and the more experienced folklorist looking at the reports
often wishes for more of the feel of the situation, the kind of
person who told the tale, the overtones and significances
which were not reported. Yet old people will talk to the
younger members of their own families in ways they never
would talk to a stranger, especially a professorial stranger. So,
taken all in all, weaknesses and strengths, I think we came up
with a clear picture of what our countrymen say about the
restless dead, a subject that has been of human concern since
the first flame flickered in a cave, since men learned to love
and face death.

This book in itself is something of a revenant. It was written under the generous terms of a John Simon Guggenheim
Memorial Fellowship in 1946–47 and laid away with the
much longer manuscript of which it is a part. It has been buried under the accumulations of a dozen busy years devoted to
many other aspects of the folk culture of New York. Now it
appears again and I hardly recognize it.

Let me also make perfectly clear my treatment of the material that my students brought to me. I have added nothing (even when the temptation was great) and have tried to keep faith with their findings while offering the reader a book of reasonably consistent tone and style. I wish that I could give you each of these stories in the words of the teller, after describing him and his intimate world. Instead, I offer a sense of the relationship of one story to another, one attitude and belief to the next. I have changed certain personal names (never place names) to avoid possible embarrassment, but the original material and all the information in our archive about collector and informant is at the disposal of the interested scholar. The names of the collectors and informants appear in the back of the book.

Finally, to save some of my readers trouble of mind, let me make it clear that I have tried, in revising this manuscript, not to put on the hat I wear as Director of the New York State Historical Association. For example, in the story of the woman who haunts the octagon house in Walton, one would get the impression that the cemetery is almost across the road. I know that is not so, but here I am concerned only with what the people say happened, and if they have confused geography or dates, I have left it their way. In short, as a folklorist I have tried to stick as closely as possible to my sources; as a historian I have gone fishing.

LCJ

Cooperstown, New York
December 31, 1958

CHAPTER ONE

Introducing the Dead

People talk of the returning dead in differing tones and varying moods. There is the man who has seen a ghost himself and knows what he has seen and would go to court and swear to the truth of his experience. There is that man's son, who has had no such encounter—but this thing happened to his father, a man who did not lie, so the truth is as he tells it. Then there is the doubter who reports the legend of the neighborhood. He would have you think he is above such

1

superstition, but often, if you press him hard or catch him unaware, you discover that really he is not so sure; a lot of strange things go on in the world and this legend is not the strangest; probably it is not so, but—. Then there is the true doubter who tells his story with a sneer and a chuckle—and frequently tells it badly. Finally, we have the sophisticated teller who is tuned only to the age of science, but for the moment, while he tells his yarn and until he has achieved his effect, would have you think him otherwise. Because he is a literate man, familiar with literary patterns, he often tells the best story of all.

I am sometimes asked what those who think they have seen ghosts have really seen. I cannot answer that with any great assurance; I can only recite an experience which helped my understanding tremendously. It happened at a time when I was not unusually interested in this type of folklore, and it is the only experience of its kind I have ever had. I was not then, as I am not now, convinced that those who die come back to earth in a sensible form, nor was my actual experience unusual at all—it has happened millions of times to others. I recount it merely because I can make this report from first hand and without any question in my own mind as to the validity of the details.

In his later years my father was a devoted gardener; March to November he spent from dawn to dusk among his flowers. His knowledge of botany and floriculture was wide and based on scientific study, which he had been carrying on as an avocation for fifty years. During the last ten years of his life I would drop in on him once or twice a week, and there was a good chance that I would find him on his knees among his flowers or in the barn working over his records or preparing plants or seeds for the ground.

He died in Albany in January, 1941, and in March I persuaded John Witthoft, then one of my students and today Chief Curator of Anthropology at the Pennsylvania State Museum, to take over the care of the garden for my stepmother. On one of those March days when the air has the softness of spring in it but the ground is still covered with snow, John and I went out to the barn to look the situation over, to see what plans had been left, what experiments were under way, what fertilizer and seeds we would need.

This was a typical city barn, divided in two rooms, one a single horse stall and the other what had been a carriage room. It was a place where I had played all through my boyhood; it was always a place closely associated with my father. We entered the small door in front of the horse stall, and I went through into the dark, big carriage room to roll back the sliding door, so we could see what was there.

As the door rolled back the room was lighted by the brilliant morning sun reflected from the snow. When I turned to look at the room, my father was sitting on a crate cutting peony roots. He wore his old work clothes, a faded shirt, and dirty pants; his ancient straw hat was stuck on the back of his head. Beads of sweat covered his brow and his shirt was dark under the arms. He kept right on working. He looked up at me, his beard white and gleaming, but his pale blue eyes were more cold and expressionless than I had ever seen them. There was neither pleasure nor anger in his face—it was merely that he was looking straight at me. And then pres-

ently he wasn't there. John had seen nothing but an up-
turned crate.

Being a product of the twentieth century I had an explanation. In a room redolent with memories of my recently
dead father, I projected from my mind his image. Emotion,
fatigue, recollection, all contributed toward the vision. This
was a psychological experience—and not a very unusual one
at that. With my training and attitudes, that is all that it
could have been, but suppose I were not a product of this
age but of an earlier and more believing one? Suppose I had
been raised in a climate of opinion which assumed as a matter

of course that for any one of a million reasons—or for no reason at all—the dead come back. Suppose members of my family, the leaders of my church and community had told me of these visits from the dead as true experiences; suppose the neighborhood in which I lived contained houses from which everyone shied away because they were haunted. . . . What then would I have seen? Then it would have been no projection from my unconscious mind, but my father's ghost, pure and simple. Not only that, but it would have been perfectly understandable, under those circumstances, for the meeting to have been far more fruitful. He might then have spoken to me, given me messages, warnings, advice which, under the circumstances, would have had tremendous meaning for me.

When one considers in how many lands and for how many centuries this would have been the accepted interpretation of what I saw, one at least pauses long enough to salute the tradition of the past and try to understand it. There is always, I tell myself, the possibility that the explanation of the centuries is right and the psychologists of my own time wrong. They have been wrong on other occasions.

For our purposes we shall, from this point forward, assume that the ages *are* right and examine the reports of the people concerning the returning dead as though we had never a doubt in our minds that what is said to have happened did happen. This is the folklorist's path.

When the dead return they adopt a wide variety of guises and forms, some in the vivid likeness of their mortal bodies, others as wraiths or lights, still others in shapes so weird and uncanny that they seem to have stepped out of drunken nightmares.

First of all, there are the living corpses, bodies which have been certified for burial and laid out in their coffins. They rise in their solemn place and act for a few moments—never for long and only once—as though the mortal spark were still alive. But, and this is important, these people are really dead and have no business acting in this fashion. Very often, I notice, those who speak of this phenomenon are from Irish background, and the stories are told as happening in both this country and Ireland.

At the wake of an Albany man named Ferris he sat up in his coffin, frothing at the mouth. Only a priest could lay his spirit to rest, but the family had great difficulty persuading one to come, for it is known that the priest who lays such a spirit soon dies himself. Finally, they tell me, a young priest came. He drew a circle on the floor and invited the dead man to step inside it. As soon as Ferris was inside it, the priest knocked him down, and then they put Ferris back in the coffin and went on with their wake. But before the year was out the young priest was dead.

Sometimes a similar incident is told as a joke. They tell of old Sean, who drank himself into his coffin; in the midst of his wake, when the good Irish whisky was passing from hand to hand, he could finally stand it no longer and rose in his coffin to shout, "What's the matter with me? Ain't I good enough to have a drink wid youse at me own wake?" But usually the animated corpse is taken very seriously.

There is an Irish telling of this theme in the family of Margaret Kelley of Cohoes, people originally from Ballinrobe and Roscommon in Ireland. It concerns the family Monaghan, who lived a century or more ago in Roscommon, a man and his wife with their twelve sons. The sons were of as many different temperaments as they were of different ages. The eldest was calm and wise, while some of his brothers were always fighting mad about something and forever making the house a howling bedlam of violence and bitterness. They lived on a farm, far from any town, and they were so poor that for several months of each year the father packed off to Dublin to get some ready cash. Those were trying times in the little farmhouse, for the din of battle continued from cockcrow to the lighting of lamps, and sometimes on into the night. The boys were expected to keep the farm running while their father was away; but their mother, who was a sweet and gentle soul, left the decisions to her sons, and they could never agree on the way the work should be done. It was the strong hand of their old man that they needed to keep peace in the place; as time went on, this became increasingly their need. One day a quarrel that had been flaming into trouble off and on for three months burst out between two of the bigger boys. It began at breakfast and continued intermittently well into the morning, first in the house, then by the barns, and finally out on the bog. It came to an end when they both lay dying.

The deep and terrible anger of their father when he returned from Dublin a few days later was directed toward his wife, a woman so weak that she couldn't protect her children from their own boyish violence, a woman who didn't deserve a dozen sons, a woman whose very presence in the house was a menace to her family. He cursed her for a weakling and a fool; he drove her from the door, calling upon God and the saints to see to it that never again would she find a place of rest, that she keep wandering over the face of Ireland though her feet be cold and though she never found a place to lay her head.

She traveled through many towns and many villages. For a spell she was down Limerick way, working now here, now there; then she went to Cork, where after a time she found work with a fine family. She had worked in that house some years, doing all the dull and thankless tasks that fall to the maid-of-all-work. Then there came an evening when the master and mistress announced that they were going out, going, in fact, to the wake being held for the brilliant and greatly beloved young priest of a parish on the far side of the city. Instead of docilely trudging back to the kitchen, the broken and defeated woman hesitated, then calling on all her courage, asked if she might be permitted to accompany them. It was made clear that they were not accustomed to taking the servants with them on such occasions, but there was a desperate pleading in her voice that prevented their persisting in their refusal. As they clattered across the city, she sat huddled in the far corner of the carriage, a bent shadow in black who spoke no word from the time they started until they left her standing outside the parish-house door. About an hour after the couple entered, Mrs. Monaghan walked in, approached the coffin, and then, after a long look at the sweet, calm face of the dead priest, knelt beside the coffin to tell the beads of her rosary.

The minutes ticked by, lengthening into hours, and still the homeless wanderer continued to pray. It was at the very

stroke of midnight that those in the room saw the strangest
sight of their lives. First they heard a stirring noise in the coffin, then they saw the corpse sit straight up. Slowly he raised
his hand and placed it on the kneeling woman's head. The
voice that had said many a mass in their hearing spoke
slowly, steadily: "Mother dear, do not weep. I who was your
eldest son have prayed for you since you left us in our youth,
and I knew that we would meet again. Your sins have been
forgiven you, and from this very moment on you will have a
place to lay your head and will never again be cold. God be
with you." The old woman sobbed out in anguish as the priest
was seen to lie back once more in the coffin. She stood up and,
leaning over, kissed her son farewell. Then she turned, stum-
bling to the floor. When they reached her, she was with her
son.

The living corpse is not a very frequent phenomenon in
American folklore. On the other hand the commonest form
assumed by a ghost is an appearance so lifelike that, unless he
is known to be dead, he passes for a living person—until he
vanishes or does something else out of the ordinary. Of
course, if you know a person is dead and meet him on the
street, or if he drops in on you one night, then there can be
no question about what manner of man he is.

Not infrequently one who is dying appears elsewhere than
his place of death at the time of his death—and that can be
very confusing. The spirit just released from the body is apparently especially active, although his presence is seldom
purposeful; he has no reason for appearing, beyond the simple pleasure of trying out his new-found power. Defoe, in

1706, wrote a classic report of such a visitation in *The True Relation of the Apparition of one Mrs. Veal,* but visits to friends and relatives just after death are not at all uncommon.

One day a woman on the Utica–Little Falls bus was telling of a family in East Schuyler who had an annual autumn visit from a city fellow who liked to help with the milking. One October he didn't come and no explanation accounted for his absence, but nobody thought much about it. Then one morning late in the fall, Henry, the old farmer who owned the place, was out milking when he felt a tap on the shoulder. He turned around to see his city friend standing by him. "Can I help you milk her, Henry?" was all he said. Henry got up and let him finish milking, thinking no more about it except that his friend had decided to come after all—Henry wasn't one of those fellows who thinks you have to waste a lot of breath talking. The newcomer milked until the pail was full, whereupon he handed it to Henry and walked to the house. At breakfast Henry took a good deal of ribbing from his family after he asked where their visitor was and told them about the milking. He didn't say a thing—not even the next week when word came that their friend had died down in New York the morning he was there milking, up in East Schuyler.

There are plenty of other stories like that: There's one about a man who was seen fixing his roof just before they brought word that he had been killed in a mine some miles away; another about a woman who was seen praying in a New York City church at almost the same time her body was taken out of the East River; and on countless farms and in city homes the dying or but momentarily dead appear to those who love them at some distance from their bodies.

In the type of oral ghost tale which is nearest to literary form, such as the stories of the ghostly hitchhiker and others of the contemporary tales (see Chapter Six), the crux and impact of the tale most frequently depends upon this ability of the dead to deceive the living into thinking that the ghost is alive. Often it is not until he vanishes that the truth is discovered.

The next degree away from reality—if we start with the solid bulk of the animated corpse, then take the lifelike ghost—is the spirit which is perfectly recognizable but is unquestionably a ghost because of its translucent and somewhat filmlike form. It is recognizable in every detail, but the observer is under no illusion about what he is facing. From this point on, ghosts become progressively less distinguishable until they seem mere rushings of air in the night.

These apparitions fall into three main divisions: First there are those characterized by whiteness; then there are those who appear as lights; finally there are the miscellaneous grotesqueries.

Artists are great ones to favor the ghost as a white figure, usually dressed in something that looks like a trailing night-dress. Actually the people report this form only occasionally. "The woman in white" is a familiar expression, but she is not very clearly defined. We hear such descriptions as a "white ghostlike shape," a "hazy figure," a "whispy white mist," and a "figure surrounded by a nimbus," but they are not much more common than animated corpses.

Many ghosts are credited with appearing as lights of various sorts. We had balls of fire which skittered about a farmhouse I once owned, and several of our country friends took a serious view of the matter. These balls of fire do act as though they are looking for something, of course, but after a while they stopped bothering us, so either they weren't ghosts or they found what they wanted. Personally, so long as the house didn't catch on fire, I didn't much care one way or the other.

A ghost that appears as an ordinary light, looking like a lantern or flashlight from a distance, which goes over the same route night after night usually has a message he wants to convey; either he wants reburial in a cemetery (this seems to be a favorite need of murdered peddlers) or he wants to point out where money is hidden. A few of the wandering dead take the form of flames or colored lights; but frequently these are not souls but supernatural warnings of a tragedy or disaster which is to appear in a locality or affect a particular family.

The routine ghosts who have no more imagination than to come back as lights and shadows seem pale and uninteresting beside the grotesque characters who choose some unorthodox form for their returns. Long before Washington Irving there were headless ghosts in York State and a sizable number are still remembered. Sometimes there is no head at all; sometimes it is carried by a horseman on his lap. On the road from Groveside to Boyntonville, farmers report that if you start off to market just before dawn, there is a chance that as you go through a patch of woods you may be held up by a whole procession of headless men walking across the road. Near Dumpling Hill an old German used to keep handy a loaded rifle in the stock of which he had placed passages of Scripture written on rolls of paper; this was a guaranty against all witches and ghosts but especially against a headless Indian he had seen in front of his house, dancing around an old stump. In Lewis County they told of a headless man who came to a certain barn and milked the cows—but it was hard to keep hired men on that farm, anyhow. Not until the barn burned did he go away. On Watch Hill, near Yorktown Heights, if you stand by a certain rock at midnight when there is a full moon, you can see a headless Revolutionary soldier step out of a crevice in the rock. Not infrequently, as we shall see, headless ghosts are the guardians of buried treasure.

Not only do bodies without heads appear, but miscellaneous parts of anatomy appear too. One of the workers in our Watervliet arsenal, for example, remembers an incident of his youth in Germany that would rivet itself into the memory of any man who had experienced it. When he was a boy, he used to wander from farm to farm to help with the harvest. So it was with a group of other workers that he lay one night in a haymow that they had filled that day. The sun was down and the weary men had climbed into the loft to get their sleep, but the time for sleep had not yet come, and they lay in the warm, sweet hay, talking and joking. The principal butt of their laughter was a lank, big-handed Bavarian named Ernst. The laughter was rough and the teasing sharp until the poor boy grew irritable and anyone with half an eye could see his temper getting out of hand. Perhaps another minute and there would have been a free-for-all there in the hay, but the excitement which came was of a different sort.

The one nearest the ladder thought someone was coming up with a lantern, and in a moment the whole gang had turned in expectation to see who was joining them. The ragging of Ernst stopped; expectation turned to terror as the group saw a brightly glowing head swim up through the hole in the loft, move swiftly among the men until it hovered above the shaking Ernst. The heavy-lidded eyes looked at him, through him; the voice was clouded and far away: "Pray, Ernst, pray for your sister's soul, for this day she was drowned." The head moved on, rose in the air, and floated silently out the open window just under the roof. There wasn't much work done on that farm the next day, especially after the neighbor came to call Ernst home for the funeral of his sister, who had indeed died as the strange messenger of the night before had announced.

In Pittstown there is a house, I am told, where on the anniversary of a murder a pair of bloody hands appears on the front door. And from the North Woods comes the story of a man whose fishing one day netted him nothing but long strands of a woman's hair. And after his wife had dried the hair out by the fire, it continued to make a sound like the dripping of water—and in the middle of the night a voice came from the hair to tell the woman of a murder and how the body must be taken from the lake and buried. Every night the dripping continued—the voice never came again—until word had been passed on to the authorities for the raising of the body. But most spectacular of all is the ghost that appears limb by limb, then head and torso, each part rolling down the stairs of the house he haunts in Poughkeepsie. Finally the parts roll together and there stands your spook. Most people don't hang around very long, looking at him. It is worth noting that only very rarely, in the folklore of our people, do the dead appear as skeletons—Hallowe'en notwithstanding.

When you see a ghost in the form of an animal, it may be either the spirit of an animal returned to earth, or it may be a ghostly human in this guise. The latter is by no means common, and very frequently when found here it comes from Italians who are accustomed to this belief in the old country. One American of Italian origin tells of a woodsman he knew who saw a ghost bulldog once, with the face and mustache of a friend of his who had recently been killed nearby. Generally speaking, of course, what seems to be the ghost of an animal is just that. Horses and dogs are the most likely to return to our world, but cows do too, and once in seven blue moons a shade of a cat will come mincing in. That seems odd to me— that cats, with all their reputation for mystery and secrecy, are not more often seen after their ninth life is closed. Horses sometimes carry ghostly riders, more often appear by themselves. One rose from her grave to help her master do a last spring plowing ("the skin was a mite loose, but it was old Dolly, all right"), while a famous trotter buried on the grounds can be heard at Matteawan State Hospital.

If a ghost is the sensible return of a soul from among the dead to the land of the living, we are put to it for a proper name for the reappearance of inanimate objects which return from the past. Often this is part of a re-enacted scene in which those objects had a part. A ghostly horse will draw a ghostly hearse to the cemetery; a train will travel down the track; a ghost will turn a grindstone that has long since been discarded. In Troy there was a little Quaker lady who liked to return to the room that had been hers when she was alive, and when she came all the furniture which had been there in her day came back too.

One phenomenon that has always interested me is the reported presence in Cohoes of the Death Coach, so well known in Irish folklore. It is a good example of the constant absorption into our American folk culture of the lore of those who came to us from across the sea. As in Ireland, the coach followed certain streets and the souls who died along its route during the day were picked up at midnight, and it was considered a great honor to live upon its circuit. The coach was sometimes called the "horseless carriage," for no horses were visible between its shafts. In the same city there was another ghostly carriage full of gay, dead young people, enjoying themselves but not the least bit interested in stopping for fresh recruits.

While many accounts of the returning dead are hazy, there are enough with sharp details to make it possible to assert that twice as many men return after death as women. One reason for this is that men are much more likely to meet their deaths violently than women, and a goodly segment of the wandering dead were murdered, killed in accidents, or committed suicide; about every third ghost met death violently.

Their age is somewhat more difficult to determine. My guess would be that the age of ghosts (they seem not to age after death) follows the normal mortality curve of a hundred years ago, with a reasonable allowance to account for the exceptional number of murders, suicides, and fatal accidents.

Since there was then an unusually high death rate among children, we observe that about one ghost in ten is under his majority, but even with this group, many were done in by violence. This is in contrast to the stories of European ghosts, where relatively few are young.

One of the striking facts about the dead is that apparently almost anybody can come back if he has sufficient reason or wants to. There are thousands of the returning dead who were just ordinary, run-of-the-mill citizens like yourself. If you had sat across the bridge table from them while they were still alive, it never would have occurred to you to say to yourself, "This is the type that haunts houses." Many of them are plain farmers or simple housewives. But businessmen, servants, industrial workers, clergymen, soldiers, and sailors are just as likely to return as horse thieves, gamblers, prostitutes, and "fellers who die bad." Jews, Catholics, Protestants, and heathens, Negroes, Indians, and white men, saints and sinners all have the same rights after death; if they want to come back, they come. These, of course, are the recognizable ghosts; there is the great multitude whom none can recognize and of whom nothing specific is known.

In all fairness ghosts have gotten an undeservedly bad name. Everybody goes about acting afraid of them and this reflects on their reputations; all this foolishness in the Sunday supplements and on Hallowe'en and a long-standing tradition has led the people to think that meeting the dead is a harrowing experience and fraught with great dangers. This is nonsense and statistically unsound. I could produce tabulations and charts to prove it isn't so. What this country needs is a

Society for the Prevention of the Defamation of the Returning Dead.

The truth is that the great majority of the dead are totally
indifferent to your values, but they do have something on
their minds that needs to be taken care of, or they have some
sort of compulsion which makes it necessary for them to come
back to old scenes. It is true, a few come back maliciously, but
much less frequently in this country than abroad. Never does
a malevolent ghost harm one who is innocent of wrong; when
one of them is violent, it is because he has good reason and I
have heard of their knocking down, whipping, beating, brand-
ing, scratching those they feel they are justified in punishing.
But a ghost almost never runs berserk, hurting innocent by-
standers; the few who are out for trouble direct it at those
who have betrayed them. If your conscience is clear, you have
nothing to worry about; even if it isn't, it may be some con-
solation to know that occasions of violence are very rare indeed. On the other hand, a great many ghosts are a nuisance,
making noises, moving furniture, letting the cat in, scaring
the dogs or horses, opening doors that are locked and shutting
blinds that are open, but these antics are more often than not
devices for getting attention. These are not the malevolent
dead, though some people are frightened by them. As we shall
see presently, many ghosts come back to do favors of various
kinds and with other generous and kindly purposes in mind
—far, far more than come back in anger.

Chapter Two

Why They Return

It would be an endless task to present the wide variety of reasons why the dead return, but perhaps a little sampling will give some idea. After examining hundreds of accounts of ghosts, it seems to me that these reasons fall roughly into five categories: they come back to re-enact their own deaths; to complete unfinished business; to re-engage in what were their normal pursuits when they were alive; to protest or punish; or, finally, to warn, console, inform, guard, or reward the living.

Why anyone would want to re-enact his last moments on earth, especially if those moments were fraught with intense inner conflict, I do not understand—yet. One old man who died sitting in a little closet off his bedroom, putting on his pants (one of the most absurd of all human postures certainly), has been seen by his granddaughters in the same closet, going through the same business more than once. In Johnstown, after World War I, a shell-shocked father came roaring out of his house one day with a razor in his hand and slashed the throat of his wife, who was standing by their fence with her baby in her arms, talking to a neighbor woman. As he ran on toward the back yard his wife started to follow him, yelling, "I'll kill you!" The moment she moved, her head dangled and she fell down dead. As soon as he saw that she was dead he cut his own throat. Blood flowed all around them. A few nights later two women saw the figures re-enacting the whole scene, and the agonizing screams chopped through the quiet of the night. The house they lived in was hardly fit for habitation because of the racket they made, and this continued despite the fact that three times priests blessed the house and yard. They kept on disturbing the peace until the house burned down.

Suicides most frequently get the urge to try again. In Glenmont, below Albany, they tell me there is a house which once belonged to the Van Rensselaers. Long ago and for some reason now forgotten, the lady of the house lost her reason and began to distrust and then hate her entire family. One day the ragged thread of her sanity snapped and she went to the attic where she burned all the valuable papers she could find and then went out on the widow's walk. There she paced up and down for a few moments before she leaped off. It is in that last moment or two of indecision and in that final leap that she is seen in our time: the unsettled pacing to and fro, the sudden jump, the hurtling body.

To a mortal mind it makes far more sense for the dead to return to complete some matter of business which was left unfinished at death than to go through the death act over and over again. Later we shall discover a considerable number of stories with this as the motivating factor, but a few examples now will set the pattern. When the dead die with something on their minds, some intention unfulfilled, some question unanswered, they often do something about it.

Down in Schoharie there was an old man who had a sprightly daughter who was being courted by a chap named Sam whom her father didn't think worth the powder to blow him to Hell. There wasn't much he could do about it; he was down sick in bed and the girl had a mind of her own. One day Sam was hanging around the house and the two men had some words. It ended up with the old man yelling out that he'd get even with the young pipsqueak somehow, some day. A few days later he died and Sam was free to see his girl as often as he wanted. One night after they had been making the plans for their wedding, he started whistling down the path for home. It was close to midnight when he saw the girl's father standing in the middle of the path with a whip in his hand, only instead of the decrepit oldster he had been when he died, he was young and strong and full of fight. He lay into Sam with his whip and Sam ran; the faster he ran, the heavier came the blows of the whip. All the way home the whip kept lashing away and Sam couldn't escape it. After he got in the house he packed up a bundle of his duds and lit out of there; the girl never saw him again. So that was a piece of business that was finished.

Farther east, near Mariaville, there was a Scot who had an argument with his next-door neighbor over their boundary line; the neighbor claimed that Sandy had moved the stone that served as a marker some distance in his own favor. After Sandy died there was even more trouble because the case went to court. And those who passed that way claimed that you could see the old Scot sitting out there on the stone, all night long, his red tam-o'-shanter cocked on his head as though he just dared anyone to lay a finger on that stone. So far as I know, nobody ever did.

Husbands and wives have their unfinished business too. They tell of a Massachusetts man who was a cussed character and made his wife's life a misery for years. She was a gentle, placid soul who let the old brute have his way and just went on being sweet about it. Time went by and neither of them changed any, right up to the day of his death. But one night after he had been gone a few weeks she woke up with a start to find him standing beside the bed. She was scared; she didn't say a word, just lay there in the darkness. The next night she woke up about the same time and there he was again. He didn't move or make any gesture in her direction; all he did was to stand there looking down at her. If she was scared the first night, she was terrified this second time. Both nights, after a while, he faded away. The third night when she went to bed she decided that if he came again she would lay aside her fear and speak to him. After all, it was only her husband,

and if she could put up with him for years on end while he was alive, she figured that there wasn't any sense in her being frightened of him after he was dead. That night he was there again. She held her breath for a minute and then she spoke.

"What do you want, John?"

"I want your forgiveness, Mary, for the bad way I treated you during our life together."

"Good heavens, John, is that all you want! You were forgiven long ago." And with that John disappeared and never came back, so far as she knew.

The shoe was on the other foot in a family up in Lowville where the wife died, never having cured her husband, Matt, of card playing. She had spent all her married life trying to persuade him by fair means and foul to give up going out with the boys to play poker. She did better after death. Old Matt's house, then being womanless, was a fine place for the crowd to gather, so for some months after he became a widower, Matt played host to his cronies. Then he began to notice that one by one they were dropping out. It wasn't until his friend Paddy was the only one left that he found out why. His wife had discovered that by appearing to each of her husband's friends on a night when he was going home alone through the swamp, she could discourage his poker playing for some time to come. They tell me she is still hanging around Lowville, and any man in that town who starts making a practice of leaving his wife home so that he can get in a little stud with the boys is liable to meet up with her on the way home—especially if he has to pass that swamp out Matt's way. Some women are just spoilsports by nature.

A very different reason brings a woman back to Walton,

and has been bringing her back for a long time. About a hundred years 'ago a woman wanted an octagon house and her husband had the plans drawn and was all ready to build it when she died. They owned a piece of land alongside a very twisting road not far from the cemetery, and after she was buried, her husband went ahead and built the house anyway. It is one of the few octagons in that section. It has a spiral staircase from cellar to cupola and other interesting details that would have pleased the lady mightily if she had ever had a chance to see it. And she tries, mind you, to get there from the cemetery to have a good look at it, but she never quite makes it. Everyone knows that the reason there are accidents there at night is that drivers see her halfway across the road and swervé to miss her, often piling into another car. But you can't blame her for trying.

Another to whom a particular building meant a great deal was the pastor of a Catholic parish who had planned for many years to repair and remodel his church. The congregation had been collecting money for that purpose and at length there was enough saved to begin the work. At that point their beloved and devoted priest died and other hands had to carry through the plans. The new priest did the best he could to fulfill the dream of his predecessor, but the details had not all been set down and when he went over the matter with the contractor, he had to guess at many of the original intentions. The workmen erected their scaffolding and started work. The first night as they were about to leave the building an elderly priest met the foreman at the door and gave precise instructions for the work that was to be done the next day. They followed his orders, and the next night, indeed every night, as the foreman was about to leave, he found the old priest at the door. It was not until some days later that the foreman had occasion to seek out the young pastor to ask some questions about the day's work which the older man had not made quite clear. What old priest was the foreman talking about? There must be some mistake, for no one besides the pastor had any voice in the changes that were to be made. At length it became apparent that the dead priest was seeing to it that his plans were carried out to the last detail, and his successor very wisely gave instructions that whatever orders he gave were to be fulfilled to the letter. The ghost continued to come each night for his brief interview until the church was finished.

There is an interesting group of stories dealing with ghostly priests who fulfill after death promises made while still alive. The basic tale is of European origin and has made itself completely at home on American soil; there is little distinction to be made among the versions which came from Ireland, Italy, and Alsace-Lorraine and those which are told of Albany, Glens Falls, and Brooklyn. Probably the story could be found among Catholics the world around, for often, I notice, it comes directly or indirectly from a member of the clergy. This is the story of the priest who died before certain masses which he had promised to say could be said, and how ultimately the mass was sung and the promise kept.

It sometimes happens that a dead priest contrives to bring to the attention of a living confrere the fact that in passing to the other side he has left obligations unfulfilled. There was a priest who took over a parish in Wellsville, for example, after an elderly and greatly beloved pastor had died. Soon he observed a curious phenomenon: every night as he lay in bed a strong light shone on the books of a certain section of the bookshelves. This became so annoying that he called in an electrician and did everything else he could think of to discover the source of this strange and unaccountable nuisance. Finally, almost in desperation, he took out all the books in that section of the shelves and went through each one, page by page. The last book in the section was the breviary the old priest had been reading when he died. In its pages the priest found a ten-dollar bill and a note requesting ten masses for the dead. Apparently they had been given to the old man, who had died before the masses could be said. After the request had been fulfilled, the light never shone again on the bookshelves.

Another and similar incident about a dead priest concerns the combination on the safe rattling each night as the successor read his office, and not until the order book was discovered within the safe and the masses said did the rattling cease. In Toledo, Canada, the dead priest appeared to one of his parishioners, whereupon she fled the church where she had gone to pray. When she told the current pastor, he advised her to go back a second time, for the dead man might have some important message for her. She followed his advice and when the old priest appeared he told her of a mass for which he had been paid but which he had failed to say. Until that mass was said, he would be unable to rest. And so the living priest said the mass and the dead priest found it unnecessary to return.

Often, however, it is the dead priest himself who sings the mass, and this is the more common European version if the examples at my disposal are a sufficient cross section to judge by. While this has been told as happening in St. Mary's Church in Glens Falls and in the Cathedral of the Immaculate Conception in Albany (where the girl who saw the dead priest say the mass left the building with her hair suddenly turned snow-white, to die a few days later), I prefer the version which concerns Visitation Parish in Brooklyn.

About thirty years ago a man fell asleep in the back of that church and was locked in for the night by mistake. Promptly at midnight he awoke. Lights had been turned up on the altar, and a priest had come out dressed in his vestments, evidently prepared to say mass. He stepped to the foot of the altar and, facing the empty pews, called out, "Is anybody here? Is anybody here?" When no answer came, the lights went out and the priest disappeared.

The poor man in the rear pew was so frightened that he had been unable to speak out and for the rest of the night he huddled in the back of the church. No sooner were the doors open in the morning than he went to the priest to tell him what he had seen. It was agreed that they would go together the following night to see if the lonely cleric would return. At the stroke of midnight the candles on the darkened altar lighted up and the priest dressed in his vestments came forward once again. Once again he looked out over the dark church and asked, "Is anybody here? Is anybody here?"

"We are here," answered the living priest.

The figure in priestly vestments began saying the mass and went through the entire ritual; then he walked off the altar, never to return. The priest explained to his awe-struck parishioner, that they had seen some priest out of the church's past who had promised to say a mass and neglected to fulfill his promise. But not even in death could he rectify his fault unless there were someone present in the church as he read the mass.

Among the Irish in Glens Falls they tell of a man who, passing St. Mary's Church late one night, saw that the lights were all on and heard the choir singing for all it was worth. The front door was locked, and that made him curious, so he climbed the outside wall and peered through the window where he recognized the priest and members of the choir and congregation, all of them former neighbors and old friends of his, each of whom lay cold and dead in the burial ground.

A woman remembers that in her girlhood in Formicola, Italy, they told of a pious woman who woke in the middle of the night to hear the churchbells ringing, so she got up directly, dressed, and went to the church. But she knew none of the congregation nor the priest. Then the woman who sat next to her explained that the priest was saying masses which he had failed to say while he was still alive and that the congregation was making up for masses they had missed while they were alive—and that the pious woman was the only living soul who had ever attended one of their services.

Nor are the Catholics the only ones who tell of ghostly congregations, for the Jews have stories to the effect that sometimes at midnight, when the synagogue is locked and dark, the dead hold religious services—only they say it backward, and should anyone from among the living be present and see that ghoulish travesty, he would leave the building forever deaf, dumb, and blind. Thus, when the parents of a small child in Smorgon, Poland, discovered that he had been locked in, the parents ran in terror to their rabbi. But he was a learned man and knew how to propitiate the dead. He formed a procession of the leading men of the congregation and, each carrying a torch, they filed to the synagogue. There the rabbi stepped to the door and knocked three times. Then he repeated certain prayers backward and abjured the spirits of the dead to leave the place of worship. His learning was the saving of the child, for when they opened the doors he came forth happy and well. He told them that he had watched the dead hold their services and when they danced in the aisles, he had danced with one of them. But no one had done him any harm, and he seemed none the worse for his experience—except, perhaps, that he was a little sleepy.

Sometimes the dead return to pick up the threads of their lives momentarily and then fade back into limbo. It is often the simple, everyday acts they seek to recapture. The machinist returns to his lathe, the patent medicine king works on in his old laboratory, the miller grinds his corn once more, the widow searches the horizon for her husband's long-lost ship, and sailors walk the shore at Sodus Bay, scanning Lake Ontario for comrades who were lost in a bad nor'wester. The dead boss of an East Chatham cheese factory used to be seen in the furnace room around midnight, leaning against a post, smoking his pipe as he had been wont to do.

The drunkard may come back for a drink, like old Jim who used to hang around the Dater Tavern on the Albany–Saratoga Road. Jim had been a very pleasant fellow, drunk or sober. He worked as hired hand at various farms in the neighborhood and spent all his money in the tavern—used to say that if he ever got a mouthful of water, it would finish him. When he was dying he looked around and, with a kind of grin on his good-natured face, begged that they bury him on the little hill in back of the tavern, so it would be real handy if he needed a drink. About ten years later the tavern was sold and made into a farmhouse. The new family would wake up in the night and hear Jim down in the living room (which had been the bar) getting his nightcap before rolling back to his little residence. The end of this story provides the irony and pathos: one day one of the daughters of the family was out walking on the hill and kicked something she thought was a white stone. But it wasn't; it was Jim's skull. It rolled down the hill and fell into the creek at the bottom. They reburied the skull and the rest of the bones in a deeper grave, but the water had passed his teeth and the damage had been done. Old Jim never came again to order drinks in the old barroom, thus ending the adventure of one of the happiest ghosts of whom I know.

The Austin family, who had many another attribute, were a musical lot. Old Joseph when he was alive was one of the best players of the French accordion in New Hampshire. One time Grandpa got a notion that his father (Joseph) would likely come to see him that night, so he set the chair out in his bedroom and waited. After a spell not only his father but his uncle Jonathan put in an appearance. The three of them had a fine time talking about the old days, and when Joseph saw his accordion he was so delighted that he picked it up and began to play. He was better than when he was alive— so good, in fact, that Grandma Austin came to the door to find out what was going on. She knew Grandpa couldn't play as well as that, but when he shouted through the locked door that it was his old man playing the contraption and when she heard her father-in-law's voice, she fled in terror. As Grandpa's father and uncle rose to go, he shook hands with them both, and they promised to return if the family kept the news from Joseph's second wife, who wasn't very popular. (Of course, Grandma couldn't keep quiet, so they never came again.) But the next morning Grandpa discovered that Joseph, the old rascal, had taken the accordion with him. I like to think of him playing it wherever he is, with all his ancient zest.

The pleasures of the Austin family point up the fact that the returning dead frequently enjoy themselves immensely. And sometimes they re-enact a happy experience of special importance to themselves. A Polish woman in Schenectady recalls the day when the lord of the estate where she was born sent her on an errand to another manor. When she arrived it was after dark, so the lady of the house suggested that she spend the night. With some hesitation she added that there was only one free bedroom in the house, but she hoped that a girl could get a restful night's sleep there. The girl had a good sleep all right, but in the morning her hostess seemed unduly solicitous as to the kind of night she had put in and was relieved when she was assured that everything had been very peaceful.

A month or so later the girl came back on another errand for her master and was told to take the same room as before. This time the night wasn't so uneventful. As she was dozing off, she heard the doorknob being softly turned. She got up and went to the door, opened it, and peered out into the hall. There was no one there, so she locked her door again and went back to bed. After a spell the door was tried again, this time more violently than before. She lit a candle, unlocked the door, and again peered out into the corridor, only to find it still empty. As she closed the door she thought she heard horses' hooves and the rolling wheels of a carriage outside her window, along the cobblestone drive. She ran to the window and peered out into the moonlight; she could see the full length of the driveway but, although she could distinctly hear the vehicle, there was nothing to be seen.

Remembering the solicitude which the great lady had

shown for her the last time she stayed in the house, the girl gathered up her courage and went to the woman's room, where she explained what she had heard in full detail. There was no surprise in the older woman's face, nor any of the disbelief which the girl had half expected. No, this was what the woman had anticipated the first time. The fact of the matter was that the girl had been sleeping in the room once occupied by a daughter of the family. A suitor who was frowned upon by her parents had come to her one night, opened the bedroom door, and then driven off with her down the driveway in his fine carriage. The daughter was never seen again, but sometimes when the moon was just right, the couple would re-enact their elopement: the turning of the doorknob, the rolling clatter of the horses and carriage. Sometimes there was a tinkling of a woman's laughter, but not this night.

There was an Irish couple whose story is told in Albany and the like of which I have never heard. One would hardly say they re-engaged in their living pursuits, although, ultimately that is what happened. They were a bride and groom, but before the crumbs of the wedding cake could be swept away, the bride had gone where there is neither marriage nor giving in marriage. The nights were sleepless for the youthful widower; he could think only of the cup of happiness they had barely raised to their lips before it was dashed to the ground and broken. As he lay bemoaning his lot, about a week after his bride's death, he realized that there was a glowing light outside his first-floor window. He got out of bed to see a girl with her back toward him, standing in the moonlight and combing her hair with a golden comb. Everything about her reminded him of his wife, but he could not be sure until she turned around. He waited, breathless, beginning to think it might be a banshee, for they too are ever combing their long tresses in the moonlight with golden combs. At last she turned; it was his wife and no mistake. The swift intake of his breath must have frightened her, for no sooner was he sure that it was she than she was gone.

All the next day he thought about this; he wondered, as have so many before him who have seen the restless dead, was this a dream? Did she come to him while he slept, yet so clearly that there was no boundary between sleeping and waking? "If she were a dream," he thought, "she will not come again just as she did last night; but if she does come again, I will grab at the comb. If the comb is in my hands when the cold light of morning comes down over these green hills, then what has come to me is no dream at all but my own Mary, back from yonder." That night he didn't so much as try to go to sleep; rather he stood hour after hour by the window noiselessly waiting. When midnight came, there was the nimbus of light again and the girl just outside his window with the gold comb in her hand, combing her hair over and over. He didn't speak, nor utter any sound, but in a flash he plucked the comb from her hand. The light vanished and his bride with it. The next night she didn't come, nor the next. He was sad, looking at the golden comb, remembering, cursing his own haste. Then one night she was there.

Tired to his very soul, he had gone to bed early with the gold comb tight in his hand, the teeth of it pressed into his palm. He woke up suddenly; the light outside the window was just dimly perceptible. No sooner was he up and out of bed than she spoke to him.

"Michael, I'm needing my comb back," and he heard the sad murmur of a meadow brook in her voice; no man who loved her could refuse her asking.

Carefully now, lest his living flesh touch her ghostly fingers —the Irish are careful about these matters—he placed the comb on a yardstick that was by him, then extended it over the sill within her easy reach. When she had it again, a smile came to her eyes and they stood together and talked, the sad-glad talk of lovers who have parted, reunited, and must again go separate ways. But she had a scheme, the whys and where-fores she could make clear to no living man; the simple fact was that there was a single chance, a long and desperate chance that she could come back to the land of the living and to him, not for a few speeding seconds, but to live out the natural pattern of her life. He was to do exactly as she told him, and he was to keep well his secret.

On Friday week there was a great parade in town to open the annual fair. The merchants, the pipers, the farmers who were going to show their fine horses, and a little band of traveling showmen—all paraded down the street while the pipers played their wild music. For none of these did the young widower have any eyes; he kept watching for the end of the line, the last horse. Then it came, a beautiful stallion, white as linen bleaching in the sun, and riding it, her head high and her eyes as proud as a queen's, was his bride. Just as she had told him to, he waited, crouching low by the road-way; then, as she came abreast of him, he dashed out from his post and circled her waist with his arms to swing her lightly

to earth. Her arms were about his neck and her lips tight-
pressed to his, for in this strange manner he had rescued her
from the shadows of the other world and she could stay with
him for a long life and a happy one.

With those who return to protest deeds of omission and
commission by the living, the commonest complaint of the
dead is that they have been buried in some out-of-the-way
place to which they object. This is a prime reason why so
many victims of murder come back to us, but all such we
shall consider in the next chapter.

Sometimes a man will vow at his death that he will come
back either as a proof of his innocence or in case his wishes
are neglected. For years there was a ghost that walked the
halls of St. Agnes' School for girls in Albany, built where
there had once been a gallows tree. It was said to be one who
had stood in that spot with the rope around his neck and
sworn that he would reappear until his innocence was established. I taught in that building one year after the St. Agnes'
School had been moved to new quarters; a great many very
odd things happened but, I'm sorry to say, no ghost appeared.
A new office building is now on the site, and while steel and
concrete do not preclude ghosts, they seldom move from one
settled habitat to another.

Out in Westmoreland a farmer named DeVinney worked
hard to leave his children a heritage of rich and fruitful earth,
but he died long before his children were old enough to take
over the management of the land. Mrs. DeVinney hesitated
for some time before she sold the farm because she could hear
in her mind's ear his deathbed vow that if the land were sold

out of the family he would come back to haunt anyone who bought it. A young couple purchased it anyway, and in a few months the wife gave birth to a child. As she lay in bed reading one day a short time after her labor, she looked up to discover Mr. DeVinney sitting at the foot of the bed. He was very good-natured about it.

"I told my wife I'd come back and haunt whoever bought this house," he said, and then he grinned at her.

The woman screamed, but before her husband rushed into the room, Mr. DeVinney had gone. Nor was that the last of him. About a month later, what with a new baby, they thought there ought to be a big family party and so all the kinfolk for miles around came over for Sunday chicken dinner. Afterward, when the dishes were done, they gathered on the front porch to have a picture taken. It was a fine picture; even the baby was just as clear as could be. And there was Mr. DeVinney peering out the parlor window; he still looked good-natured about it.

Protesting ghosts are very often parents who go on trying to direct their children's lives even after death has parted them. The kind of parent who would not let his child work out his own salvation usually has the kind of child that never will learn anything anyway. There was a miserly couple out East Schodack way who had pinched and saved until they were eighty and all the fun had long since gone out of their lives. He "died of meanness and shortly after his wife died from eating moldy crackers." But their daughter found that all the poor-mouth talk she had been hearing for sixty years was foolishness; to her great amazement she came into a neat sum of money. No one in his right mind would have said that she painted the town red or spent the money like a drunken sailor, but according to her parents' standards she went hog-wild. And they made their objections very evident: they rapped on the walls at night; they bumped around the place so that nobody could get any sleep. Every once in a while her father would appear, floating up and down the stairs, white whiskers and all. Matters got so bad that she rented the house and moved away. This apparently confused her parents, for they kept right on haunting the house, while she went else-where to spend their money on simple pleasures they would have considered sheer madness. But they didn't follow her; they just made it very difficult for her to get any rent out of the house: tenants didn't stay overlong.

Another ghost had quite a different effect upon his grown son, with far more serious results. There was a very wealthy man down near Rye in Westchester County who had violated all Ten Commandments, with the possible exception of mur-der, which no one had ever proved. As his last hour ap-proached, he began to worry about his son and heir, who was a chip off the old block. If the father had learned anything, it was that one had to pay bitterly for the kind of life that he had led, and he wanted the younger man to avoid paying the price if possible. They had a long talk in which the father's fears were thoroughly explored. At the last moments he turned to his son and said, "I shall be watching you every minute of every day. If you step over the bounds into mortal sin, I shall return and make you suffer for it."

At first the son behaved very well, for his father's threat was constantly in his mind, but toward the end of the first year his financial affairs went from bad to worse. He was in danger of losing everything he owned—house, investments, his father's entire estate. There was, so far as he could see, only one way of escape: embezzlement. There was an opportunity and one day he took it.

That night he awakened to hear a strange sound; while it drew closer he tried to identify it. It was the sound of chains just outside his bedroom door. Chains are very rarely rattled by our native ghosts, but once in a while the old-country ways crop up. In terror he yelled for his butler, but when the servant came the noise ceased. The next night he ordered all the doors and windows closed and locked. He decided to stay up all night, waiting. Shortly after midnight he was just beginning to doze when the clanking rattle of the chains came again, nearer and nearer. He screamed for the servants, but by the time they arrived he had fainted.

The following night the police were asked to send a detail to watch the premises, though in his heart he was certain that no mundane law force could capture the rattler of the chains. He took one of the largest dogs from his kennel up to his room with him. Once more he ordered all the doors and windows locked and he checked the window in his room himself. He sat down by the fireplace, the only cheerful sight in a house pervaded with fear. Suddenly he looked at the dog: the beast was standing up, staring at the window. The man felt a little breeze, and then out of the corner of his eye he saw the curtain flutter. For a long time he did not dare turn around; then, in a burst of courage he did. Just inside the window stood his father. When the servants found him he was unconscious on the floor. The dog was dead.

They took the fellow to the hospital where the doctors told

him there was nothing wrong with him at all. He was in an advanced state of hysteria and insisted that his father would come for him again. On the fourth night, the first after he got to the hospital, the nurse had no sooner left his room than the whole floor was electrified by a bloodcurdling scream coming from his room. Two or three nurses and an intern rushed in to quiet him before he had the hospital in an uproar. But it was quite unnecessary; he lay dead on the floor beneath the window which was unaccountably open.

I have also heard of a mother whose post-mortem interest in her daughter's private life led to quite a different ending. There was a marriage and it had ceased to be a good marriage. Though the couple lived under the same roof, they went their separate ways. Then the wife's mother was taken ill and came to live with them. The wife gave up her job to take care of her mother, with whom she shared the guest room. After a few weeks the older woman died and was buried, but her daughter continued to use the guest room. One night, just as she was drifting off to sleep, she felt her bed move as if it had been poked. She thought it was her little dachshund, and without opening her eyes, she said, "Down, Fritz!" When the bed moved a second time, she sat up to scold the dog. But it wasn't Fritz at all; instead, beside the bed was a bright light, in the center of which stood her mother.

"Get up, Alice," said her mother, and Alice obeyed. Alice had always obeyed when her mother spoke.

Her mother held out her hand and Alice took it. As she did so, a chill ran up her arm, completely numbing it. Her mother led her quietly out of the guest room and down the hall as far as her husband's bedroom door. There she gave her daughter a look both penetrating and meaningful, after which the mother was slowly consumed by the bright light, and then that too faded.

Alice considered this a command from a better world. So she opened the door and went in; after that, they used the guest room for guests.

A constant source of discontent among ghosts is a burial not to their liking. Those lying in hidden graves or unblessed ground are universally restless. There is a story from Poland told here in New York of a woman who suffered, not for herself, but for her child. Between two Polish villages ran a road beside which was a cemetery. There came a time when anyone driving or walking along the road was likely to be joined by a strange woman who appeared from nowhere. If her companion was quiet, she went with him as far as the edge of the next town; if he spoke to her, she vanished immediately. This became such a common occurrence that nobody thought about it, one way or another. But there was one man who was not so stoical as the others. He wanted to know why this woman couldn't rest in her grave like a respectable person, minding her own business.

One day as the woman joined him he put his thumb and index fingers inside his belt, and this, for reasons which I cannot explain, kept her from disappearing when he spoke to her. She begged him to release her, but he asked, "Why do you not lie in your grave and take your rest? What is it that keeps you forever wandering between these towns?" Then she told him of her unbaptized baby, buried in a far corner of the cemetery, who would not let her rest. If the living wished to do her a real kindness, then for the love of God, go find the little grave with its cross made of tiny white stones and have the priest bless it so that she could sleep as a dead woman should. In sorrow and pity the man released her and went straightway to the priest. Together they found the little grave overgrown with weeds. They cleared away the brush and the priest blessed the grave, and then they went their separate ways. The next time the man came to the village, the woman appeared for the last time to any living soul, to thank him for bringing her peace and quiet.

It is a well-known fact that a person who loses a leg in an accident is liable to feel cold or dampness in that leg if it is buried too near the surface of the ground. A more acute problem comes after death.

A neighbor of Michael Welch, when he lived back in Ireland, lost his leg in an accident. Between the shock and his grief over the loss, it wasn't six months before he was a dead man. A few mornings after the funeral Mr. Welch and his mother were sitting over their morning cup of tea when the door opened and the widow came rushing in with a wild tale about her husband appearing to her the night before. The Welches put it down to the hard time she'd been having and the bad way she was in. But the next morning, and the next, she came back with the same story. There was something wrong, or her man would never in the wide world keep pestering so. So they told her to speak up sharp and plain to him if he came again, saying, "In the name of God, what do you want?" The next night he came again, and what would he be wanting but his leg? So they went out and dug it up and buried it with his body. That was all the poor fellow was after; from that time on, he rested easy and was no more trouble to anyone.

In a similar story, many people in a Polish village saw the revenant at different times shuffling through the streets in a brown coat with red binding and with slippers on his feet. The priest was finally consulted, and he suggested that if the man's position were changed he might rest easier. So they dug up the coffin, to discover that the body was lying on its left side. They changed him over to his right side, nailed up the coffin, and reburied it; and the man was never known to walk again.

This matter of digging up the body to make it more comfortable, or at least to change its position, reaches a kind of ultimate point in a Russian story about a woman who hung herself. Out of sheer malice she then got into the habit of going around the neighborhood at night letting all the geese loose. Some got lost; others were killed. This went on until her former neighbors decided that steps had to be taken. As soon as the priest gave permission to dig up the body, the whole village trooped to the cemetery. They soon had the coffin open. The woman's chin had been forced down on her breast by the combined effect of a broken neck and a small coffin. With the kindest intentions in the world, they chopped off her head with an axe someone had brought along, set her head between her knees, nailed up the coffin, and replanted it. After that the geese stayed in their pens and nobody saw the woman wandering about any more.

The dead have as great a variety of worries as the living and are as irrational about them. Of course, sometimes their concern derives from folk beliefs which have been forgotten.

Once, for example, there was an Irish farmer who had spent a full year mourning the death of his wife; but feeling at last the call of the living stronger than that of the dead, he asked a neighbor's daughter to fill the vacant place in his home. The lass agreed and the banns were read at mass for the first time. That very Sunday night he returned home from the fireside of his betrothed and climbed into bed with the feeling that soon again life would be warm and full, a great change indeed from the deep emptiness that filled his house.

He fell asleep, only to awaken suddenly, feeling himself shaken roughly by the shoulder. He sat up in bed. There beside him stood his dead wife looking down at him with tears in her eyes. He spoke her name, begging her to tell him why she wept and why she had returned. Her complaints came pouring over him like a cascade of tears. He had treated her shamefully, leaving her to walk the earth of nights barefooted; the night air was cold and the ground was cold, and her heart was colder yet, what with her husband's hard neglect. Never once had he thought to sprinkle her shoes and stockings with holy water, nor had he given them to some poor needy woman among the living in her name and in her memory. Now into her very house, into their marriage bed, he was to be bringing a new wife to take her place, and like as not she would be the one who would be prancing about in the fine shoes and stockings that had been left behind.

Solemnly the husband promised that he would do as his wife wished, and with his promise she faded from the room. At the first crowing of the cock, he dressed, took his wife's shoes and stockings under his arm, and set out upon the highway, walking thoughtfully until he spied a bent, old hag whose palm stretched forth for alms. They talked a while, and when he lightheartedly went back to his farm, he had the beggarwoman's promise that the shoes and stockings she had received in the dead woman's name would be worn to church for three successive Sundays and each time would be sprinkled with holy water. And she must have kept their bargain, for never again did the dead wife return. The young man entered into his new marriage with a clear conscience and the tacit blessing of the dead.

An occasional ghost seems intent upon the protection of certain ones among the living. One girl remembered a dead aunt who walked home from work with her each night, and in both Rensselaer and Haverstraw a protective ghost would appear in the form of a black dog to shepherd honest working girls at night. A rather touching story of a mother who carried her share of the burden of raising children after her death also comes from Rensselaer. The mother of five small children died and in a short time her husband remarried. Now, occasionally a dead wife will make life unbearable for her successor, but this woman apparently appreciated the fact that the children's new stepmother was doing everything in her power to give them a good home and affectionate care. When, in due time, the second wife bore two children, there was a great deal of work for one woman to do and very little to do it on. She did her best for the whole family, but there were so many little children, so many faces to wash, so many clothes to keep clean, so many dishes to be done three times a day that she never could catch up on all the nagging details of domestic life. It was at about this time that the first wife began to return. They would hear her about midnight down in the kitchen. In the morning the dead woman's children would be washed spick-and-span, and on arising even their hair would be combed, their clothes would be freshly prepared and laid out for them, making life a little easier for the woman who was taking her place.

Death has many messengers to warn the living of its approach: birds fly against the window, dogs howl, there are rappings on walls, and strange dreams disturb one's rest. But sometimes the dead themselves return to announce that one of the living is soon to join them. This comes most often, not to the one who will die, but to one close to him. A dead mother will appear to her daughter to say, "I have come for Papa." And a day or two later he goes with her. Sometimes it is less specific than that: the very appearance of a ghost in the form of "a white lady" or "a beautiful lady," who is present for a little while and then disappears, is enough to convince those who see her that she comes as a warning of death for someone.

Usually the people do not know who the mysterious woman is (it is seldom a man) who comes to warn them, but in Pancake Hollow they knew perfectly well: it was Jemima Wilkinson. Pancake Hollow is in the Pang Yang settlement between Highland and New Paltz, on the ridge above the Hudson River. Someone once said, "I've often been to Pang Yang, but I never knew exactly which place was it when I was there," and this is a comment I understand. For I was taken there once by my late friend, Warren G. Sherwood, poet, historian, gravedigger, and native of Pancake Hollow.

It was an autumn day, cold and windy, and the leaves were

mostly gone from the trees as we trudged through the woods, Warren, my eldest son, Peter, who was ten at the time, and I. Down roads long in disuse, through overgrown paths, we trudged, Warren talking incessantly about the old days as he knew them when he was Pete's age. At length we paused in the woods before a long-forgotten stone wall.

"Well," he said, "this is it."

I looked about me at the second growth, the underbrush, the blowing leaves and wondered what he meant. Then the stone shells which had once been small houses and barns began to come into focus. There were a dozen, maybe more of them, a little settlement with trees growing inside the roofless squares. Once this woods had been a village, founded in 1800 by Connecticut families intending to go far west into Yates County, where Jemima Wilkinson, the Public Universal Friend, had begun a New Jerusalem near Penn Yan on the shores of Lake Keuka. Jemima Wilkinson was one of the off-beat religious leaders who found refuge in New York State in the nineteenth century. She had once been desperately ill, and her old soul died and a new consecrated spirit inherited her body, destined to proclaim, "News of Salvation to all that would Repent and believe in the Gospel." Out in the west country among the Finger Lakes, her followers built her a noble house that still stands and the rich fields made the colony prosper.

But not all her followers reached that promised land. One group from Connecticut got no farther than Ulster County, where they bought lands and called their cluster of stone houses Penn Yan Settlement, known eventually as Pang Yang.

Jemima was not unmindful of these people nor of their

descendants. A few hours before one of them was to die, she would appear on the road, serene, comforting, dressed in gray, as she is in the two portraits of her which still exist. She came to claim her own, and they knew her in that place as the Gray Lady, never speaking her real name, perhaps lest strangers misunderstand.

Sometimes the dead return to make the first announcement of their passing to those who love them. A girl appears by her father's bedside, almost at the moment that she died a hundred miles away. A mother is sleeping soundly when the bed is shaken until she sits up and turns on the light. There is her son who works on the railroad as a brakeman, dressed in his blue-checkered hat and his blue overalls, just as he was when he went out on his run a few hours before. Very quietly he tells her that he has slipped and fallen under the train and been killed. Her first impression is that she has had a bad dream, but she is certain that this is not so. Early in the morning they bring home his body and tell her how he had slipped on the icy ladder as he climbed from one car to the next.

Strange lights are not uncommon warnings of death, but it is sometimes believed that the light is itself a ghost. A case in point is the tradition of the Goodell family in which a ghost light acts much as a banshee might in Ireland, coming whenever one of the family, absent or present, is about to die. Whether or not the Goodells still live north of Little Falls I do not know, but a generation ago a family named Murphy were their next-door neighbors, and it is from them that I have the tale. One evening Isabel Murphy was waiting for her brother Harry to return from town, and when he drove in the yard she went to meet him. He was very excited and pointed out into the field next to the house where there was a curious light, looking more like a lighted birthday cake than anything else, and it was moving. As they watched, it disappeared into Goodell's woods.

Harry had first seen it when some distance down the road and had thought it was the single headlight of a car. He had pulled his horse over to the side and stopped, lest the beast become frightened and bolt. When the car failed to materialize, he drove closer to discover that there was a light in the field, and that it was not being carried by anyone but was moving about under its own power.

About nine the next morning Mr. and Mrs. Goodell arrived, and that in itself was unusual, for it is a rare day when a farmer and his wife go calling in the middle of the morning. They had heard about the light and wanted all the details. When Harry told them all he knew they shook their heads as though he had confirmed all their fears. Then they settled down to explain why they were so concerned and what they thought the light meant.

The Goodells, it seemed, had been in that neck of the woods since before the Revolution and when the Indians attacked Cherry Valley in 1778, twenty miles to the south, to burn and massacre, one white man had been able to escape to the north and warn them that there was danger abroad. Thus they were prepared when the Indians came and there was no such catastrophe as took place to the south. But ever since, whenever one of the descendants of the original Goodell family was about to die, this same messenger, now in a ghostly, lighted form came to give them warning.

This explained the concern of the Murphy's neighbors, and

undoubtedly it also explains why they were not greatly surprised when a sister of the family, who was recovering nicely from an appendicitis operation in a nearby hospital, died that afternoon.

There are other stories of lights, but I know an even stranger one about shadows. In good truth, there is no ghost in it, but ghost or not, this is where it belongs. There were once three friends from Nyack who went hunting on Hook Mountain. There was a fine, full, harvest moon and they went out when it was high to make their kill—game laws notwithstanding. As they stood in the bright moonlight in an open patch on the mountainside, they were suddenly struck by a remarkable fact. Of the three, standing side by side, only two of them cast shadows. When John realized that there was no shadow for him, he was terrified, broke up the party, and went back to camp. The next day he was still unnerved, so they gave up the plans for hunting and went home.

A few days later they met for an evening at John's house to play a little pinochle. While they were playing they thought they heard something in the cellar, and their host went down to see what the disturbance was. As he stood up he dropped a card, and when his friends glanced at it, they saw it was the ace of spades. They looked at each other and both of them were unable to hide their fright. But soon they heard their friend's footsteps on the stair, and then they saw his shadow, cast from the light in the cellar. They supposed he was on the top step, but just at that moment they heard a heavy thud at the foot of the stairs, and when they rushed to see what the matter was, they found John on the cellar floor, quite dead.

He had never even put a foot on the first step before death met him.

It is not always of death that the dead warn; sometimes it is the danger of death, from which they come to protect the living. There was the night watchman in a tannery in Callicoon of whom they tell that one bitter cold night he just decided it wasn't worth while to make his rounds and that he would stay in his comfortable chair by the stove. It was then that a silent, white figure appeared before him. After that, the fire didn't seem so cozy, and he thought he might as well go make those rounds. Just as he closed the door behind him, the whole building collapsed from the weight of too many hides that had been piled high in the upper rooms that afternoon. That's one case, and the headless brakeman is another.

There was once a bummer brakeman named Tolley, who, like all bummers, never worked long on any one line. Whenever he decided to change runs, he'd get a ride in the crummy (caboose) to the place he wanted to go. This one time he was in the crummy, waiting for a friend of his, who was the regular brakeman on that run, to come back down from his inspection of the cars. It was a cold, rainy, spring night, and Tolley was just thinking that it was a terrible night for his friend to be climbing along the top of the cars when the train hit a washout at a curve on the tracks and the first dozen cars were derailed. Tolley went out to look for the brakeman and found him with his head cut off, lying between two cars. They picked up what was left of the body and put it in a baggage car, but they couldn't find the head anywhere. Tolley went back up the line to warn any train that might be following them, and as soon as the track was repaired they went on again.

Tolley settled down after that. He became a fireman, then an engineer, but he always tried to avoid the run where the accident had happened. A while after he became an engineer, he was assigned to that same run, over his protest. But that was what they gave him and he had to take it and like it. By then, trains were traveling a lot faster than they had been when he was a bummer brakeman, but whenever he came to the spot where his friend had lost his head, he slowed the freight down in spite of himself, especially on rainy nights.

That's the way matters stood for several years. Then one wet March night as he approached the fatal curve, he suddenly saw a red light on the track. He cracked the air and brought the train to a grinding stop. He told the fireman to go ahead and investigate, but the fireman came back to report that there was no light to be seen. Not satisfied, Tolley went up the track himself to investigate. As he left the cab he saw the red lantern bobbing above the track. His own white lantern was swinging by his side as he walked. He kept his eyes on the red light, and as he drew near the spot he saw what appeared to be an old-styled, red-globed lantern, faintly illuminating the lower part of a body clad in the regulation blue overalls of a brakeman. Running forward, Tolley called out excitedly, "What's the matter? What's the matter?" Since he got no reply, he raised his lantern to see why the other fellow didn't answer him. The reason was easily discovered: the body ended at the neck. Then there was nothing out there on the track but the horrified engineer and the howling March wind and the rain that was beating down in torrents. Tolley walked on up the track a little farther, because he was sure that there had been a reason for what he had seen. And there it was, just around a sharp bend: a boulder that the spring rains had loosened so that it had rolled onto the track. It was too large for the crew to remove, and they had to wait for the wrecking crew to get there. Of course, the fellows on the wrecking crew howled with laughter when they heard the story of the headless brakeman, but, considering the state of his nerves, Tolley exhibited exceptional patience in pointing out to them that the headlights of the locomotive would never have shown him the boulder in time to prevent another wreck. That was Tolley's last run; the next morning he handed in his resignation.

Not infrequently, ghosts return to convey specific information, and we shall meet a number of such stories in the pages ahead, but one example will suffice here. It is from Poland and was told by the same grandmother who heard the ghostly couple eloping when she was a girl.

It concerned the death of the noblewoman who had been managing the family estate in the absence of her son, who was abroad. After the old lady was buried, the servants discovered that no one could enter her bedroom because the minute they opened the door flames shot up, forming a wall within the room. These seemed to do no harm, and as soon as the door was closed, they ceased to burn. It was, they decided, a business with magic in it. There was a servant girl in the household who had been devoted to the old lady and was afraid of neither man nor devil. While the other servants gathered against the far wall opposite the door, the girl opened it and plunged through the flames. There in the center of the room sat the dead woman, quietly spinning. She had been waiting for the lass; she had messages she wanted delivered to her son as soon as he returned. He was to pay all the debts and wages which she had left unpaid at the time of her death. She left word where he would find the records and accounts which she had hidden away shortly before her brief illness. A day or so later the son came home, and after he had done as his mother requested, the flames no longer sprang up in her room and life went on its natural course.

These then are the principal reasons for the dead to return; most ghosts are harmless enough, it must be admitted, and some of them very well intentioned indeed. Years ago, I made a statistical count of the moods displayed by American ghosts. Thirteen percent of them were in a very unpleasant frame of mind, 29 percent couldn't have been nicer, and 58 percent were completely indifferent to human values of good or bad. Now that these results are written down they look rather silly, but no sillier than lots of other people's statistics.

CHAPTER THREE

*Haunted
Houses*

If you grew up in a reasonably small town or one of those static sections of a city, you ought to be able to recall the haunted house that was in your neighborhood. Perhaps it was a place where the families quickly moved in and moved out because strange things happened which could not be explained on rational grounds. Perhaps it was a dilapidated, empty old place, where at night the window blinds banged against the walls. Certainly the windowpanes were raggedly broken, there was an overgrowth of weeds and lilac bushes that isolated it from the other houses, and only the very brave or very foolhardy went near it at night. I remember well a house of this sort from my boyhood and how I tried to imagine what goings on had brought it to its strangely frightening state. It has taken me many years to find the answer, but I think that now I could hazard a reasonable guess.

First of all, when the dead decide that they have reasons for going back repeatedly to a particular house (and, of course, that is what we mean by a haunted house), they are prone to be noisy about it and the variety of their noises is remarkable. You wouldn't believe all the things that people hear!

The dead are a heavy-footed lot, for all their incorporeity. They are upstairs or in the attic, or they are downstairs in the cellar, or they are on the stairs, going up or down. Not just once, mind you—that could be your imagination—but over and over again they come; not just for one family of occupants, but for successive families until the house has a bad reputation and nobody will rent it. It always sounds silly to the outsider who has never heard footsteps in the middle of the night, but those who have seldom get used to the sound —even when they know it is only one of the dead.

Chains, which English ghosts seem to fancy, are rarely heard in our country, but the dead make plenty of other noises: they moan and screech, speak in muffled voices, rap on tables, roll apples in the cellar (though when you go down to see, the apples are in their baskets), knock on doors, thump and hammer, play the piano, wind clocks, and now and then let off a terrific blast, like a rifle shot. Of course, these aren't the only noises the dead make, but these are the ones that occupants of really haunted houses may expect.

For some reason, the dead seem to be especially interested in doors and windows. Doors in their houses are opened by no earthly hands; they slam shut when there is no wind blowing; they resist all mortal effort to keep them locked or latched. The dead are a persistent lot and will go to great lengths to keep things the way they want them. Henry Austin tells of a house his grandfather lived in on Piercefield Hill where the door from the kitchen to the woodshed would never stay shut. A man had been murdered there, years before, and that fellow wanted the door open, but the Austin family wanted it closed. It became a struggle to see who would win. Finally Mr. Austin shut the door and drove a good-sized spike into it, nailing it to the casing. They figured that would fix the dead man and they sat down in the kitchen to see what he would make of a spike. About half an hour later that spike flew out of the door and was driven right into the opposite wall. Then the door opened its wonted six inches. That same house had a window shade which the dead man wanted up but the family wanted down. At four thirty every afternoon it went up, whether they liked it or not. Mrs. Austin tried wiring it down once, but it just ripped to pieces and went up. Finally the Austins had to give up the place, and after subsequent tenants had even more trouble, the owner burned the place down.

Windows can give a lot of trouble. Sometimes it is the shutter—like the one in the Hardenberg Mansion which will never stay shut no matter what they do to it because the old colored woman must keep an eye on the young ones of the family who played in the yard when she was alive.

Sometimes the whole window falls out. On the state road near Alder Creek there was, up to twenty years ago, a house with a front window that they had to keep boarded up because every time they put a new window in, it fell out as soon as dark came. Once there had been a roaring good party there and in the excitement one of the boys had been thrown out that window and killed. He continued to resent it.

Furniture comes in for attention. There used to be a house up in Waterford, in back of St. Mary's Church, that was empty for about twenty-five years, except for an occasional family that tried to make a go of living in the place. The trouble was that as soon as they got in and arranged the furniture they would wake up next morning to find it entirely rearranged to suit the dead. This would go on until the family would decide that they were going to live where they could have their possessions where they wanted them.

Another annoying habit of ghosts, and a common one too, is to pull the covers off the living while they sleep. When you combine this with other manifestations, it can make life unbearable. Put yourself in the place of the families that rented a house near Crescent. No sooner would they doze off at night than their covers would be flipped right off the bed. If they were retrieved, it happened again. Next, the front door, which had been carefully locked, would swing open without any cause. It wasn't until they found a skeleton by the old spring near the house that these annoyances stopped. Of course, finding it isn't enough—you have to give it a decent burial. Then the dead can rest.

At that, they didn't have nearly as hard a time of it as an Italian family who moved to Port Byron a generation ago. The only home in town they could afford to live in was a little place which the landlord admitted was haunted before they rented it. Early each evening they would hear noises in the cellar; then about midnight the shadow of a man would glide across the wall of the upstairs bedroom. In the morning the family would awaken to find their blankets outside the window. During the two or three years they remained in that house, they would sometimes have to stay up because he was making so much noise in the cellar. At midnight when his shadow came, they would plead with him to quiet down, but it never did any good. Finally, in desperation, they burned down the house and moved to a little shack on the muckland.

Strange lights appear in haunted houses to puzzle and terrify those who try to live there and, if the place has been abandoned, those who pass by. These appear in various ways and under differing circumstances. In Port Leyden there is a house where the old man who died there still walks about the place at night with a lantern in his hand. The widow of a railroad man who had been killed in a wreck had to move out of their house in Clayville because strange lights flickered through the rooms all night long. After a girl was killed in the attic room of an Albany house, the people saw lights in her window, though the house was quite empty. Outside of Schenectady there is a house where lights have appeared ever since the owner died before he could finish telling neighbors where he had buried his money. The lights always appear in the bedroom where he died, and afterward they find the front door ajar, no matter how securely it has been locked.

Waterford, which stands at the terminus of the Barge Canal and has been the scene of many a strange sight, natural and supernatural, tells a pathetic story of domestic strife which provided the town with a light-haunted house long years after it had fallen into decay. About 1900 there lived in a poor little place by the waterfront a young carpenter and his wife and two children. His poor health—he had tuberculosis, as it turned out—made it hard for him to keep a job and encouraged his parents, an abnormally mercenary and avaricious pair, to demand that he sign over to them the title of his home. They made life miserable for him and undoubtedly their nagging hastened his death. But shortly before his death he warned his parents that if they did anything which harmed his wife and children, or if they made things difficult for them, he would haunt them as long as they lived.

No sooner was their son dead than his parents began to pull legal tricks and before the poor widow knew what had happened, her in-laws had possession of the house and had dispossessed her and their grandchildren. Because it needed considerable repair, the new owners couldn't rent it. They locked the doors and closed the shutters to wait for a tenant. But no tenant ever came because soon the neighbors began to see lights playing through the chinks of the shutters, and those who passed at night could see the lights waver and weave within. It wasn't long before people tended to walk on the other side of the street and word went out that the son was back to make good his threat. Little wonder that it fell into decay until it tumbled to the ground. But even during those later years, after it had become utterly untenantable, the light was still to be seen on occasion through the breaks in the walls and the warped casements. When at last the roof fell in and the walls collapsed, there were no more lights. But never a cent did the greedy ones get from their chicanery, and so, I suppose, their son had his vengeance.

When a place is subject to a wide variety of ghostly pranks, we say it suffers from *poltergeists,* the mischievous spirits of the dead. Now it is the plan and purpose of this book to deal in folklore, not attested psychic phenomena, but I am going to deviate from that plan for a few pages to report on two experiences with poltergeists, one occurring twenty-five years ago, the other in the winter of 1958.

In 1934 *Harper's Magazine* published an article called "Four Months in a Haunted House." It was signed with the pseudonym of "Harlan Jacobs," but the author was a professor of mine at Columbia, a very kind but practical, hard-headed scholar who vouched for the truth of every word of his article. Knowing him, his word was beyond question. Furthermore, he is not a believer in the supernatural in general, nor in ghosts in particular.

One summer in the 1930's Mr. and Mrs. "Jacobs" rented an isolated cottage on Cape Cod so they could do a job of writing they had mapped out. In view of what happened, it is interesting to note that although the house was nine years old it had never been occupied. The first night Mrs. "Jacobs" heard tapping on the brick walk outside her window, as though made by a man with a cane. The next night they both heard it. When they went outside with a flashlight, it stopped, nor was man or beast to be seen and there was no place anything could hide.

More than fifty times during the ensuing weeks they heard the same sound, always at night, usually about ten o'clock but not every night. When Mr. "Jacobs" hid outside, it did not come; when he waited just inside the door, the sound ceased the moment he opened it. And there were other inexplicable sounds. As he got into bed and turned off the light, he would hear a box of matches fall, a newspaper blow across the floor, a rolling pin bang on the floor and roll to the wall. But each time when he turned on the light, nothing was there.

They were pestered by a "universal click" which seemed to come at all hours of the day and night, sounding like the clicker a lecturer uses when calling for a new slide. To make sure it was not insects, they went over the house almost board for board. No insects. Then there were footfalls, upstairs and down, whichever place the "Jacobses" were not currently occupying.

One night Mr. "Jacobs" went into a garage attached to the house, which he used as a place to store his reference books. He was attacked by a vast swarm of moths, but when he reported this to his wife and she returned with him to see for herself, there was not a sign of one single moth. This room had a concrete floor, metal roof, and, except for the door to the house, had been shut tight all summer. Parenthetically, one might point out that in Cornwall, England, in Russia, and among certain American Indian tribes it is believed that souls frequently return as moths or butterflies.

Then there was the "grand piano smash," a terrific noise from the garage. Inspection showed nothing amiss.

A lawyer friend, his wife, and daughter came to visit. The lawyer was told about all this and was scornful; the wife and daughter were told nothing. But they all heard these sounds, although during their visit the "Jacobses" did not.

There was no explanation for all this, not even a local legend. All we have is a meticulous report from a man we can believe.

At least the "Jacobses" were permitted to suffer their indignities in private, but the Herrmann family of Seaford,

Long Island, had to share theirs with the world. In the latter part of February, 1958, the Herrmanns' difficulties were in every paper and on every radio and television station in the country day after day, for theirs was the "House of Flying Objects."

Mr. James M. Herrmann, an Air France employee, his wife, his thirteen-year-old daughter, and twelve-year-old son live in a modern housing development thirty-five miles from New York City. One afternoon in February, 1958, several bottles containing various types of liquid in various rooms of the house began to pop off their screw caps and jump about, among these a bottle of holy water, others of shampoo, medicine, liquid starch in the kitchen, and bleaching fluid in the cellar. Three days later, at approximately the same time in the afternoon, half a dozen other bottles in different rooms of the house blew off their tops and fell to the floor. This happened time and again in the days to follow.

On Sunday of the next week Mr. Herrmann was talking to his son, who was brushing his teeth, when a bottle of medicine moved a foot and a half in a southerly direction along a sink top and smashed into the sink. Then it happened to a second bottle going in a westerly direction.

They called in the police and while the patrolman questioned the family, more bottles popped. Detective Joseph Tozzi was assigned to the case and you couldn't have chosen a man less sympathetic to explanations which suggested the supernatural. Bottles kept popping and spilling. On the fifteenth of February the bottle of holy water spilled for the fourth time; when Mr. Herrmann picked it up it was warm to his touch, though this was the only time any of the bottles were warm.

Letters poured in on the family from all over the country, for by this time the press services, radio, and television were having a heyday. The sincere, the troubled, the crackpots, and the publicity seekers deluged the Herrmanns with advice.

One day a porcelain figure took off from a table, flew twelve feet, and fell against the wall—this while Detective Tozzi was in the house. They checked every possible scientific explanation that was suggested. An ink bottle, a sugar bowl, another porcelain statue sailed through the air all in one evening; shortly thereafter the Herrmanns went to the house of a relative for a few days. Nothing happened. They returned and two days later the sugar bowl misbehaved again; this time it broke. Two days later an eighteen-inch statue of the Virgin sailed twelve feet from a dresser top to hit a mirror on the opposite wall, denting the frame but breaking neither the glass nor statue. When the radio fell off its table and slid fifteen feet across the floor and a bookcase fell over on its face, the peak of the disturbance was reached. It is interesting, I think, that as time went on more and more people suggested *Poltergeisterei* as the cause. There were a great range of other explanations, all of them disproved by hard-headed and very alert Detective Tozzi.

I have not recounted the stories of the "Jacobses" and the Herrmanns because I wish to claim that either house was haunted or that poltergeists were responsible. Rather, the stories serve to show the kind of experience people in our time occasionally do go through. If happenings of this sort take place in a climate of opinion where ghost lore is generally accepted, then there is no other explanation possible—except, of course, witchcraft. Personally I have no explanation for either of these cases, but I think even the most realistically minded can accept them at face value.

In the folklore about poltergeists there is usually an explanation for their presence, unlike the examples you have just read. For example, there was a house in Schenectady which was once a dive. Unfortunately some of the girls were un-co-operative and ended up buried in quickly dug graves in the cellar. One night there was a brawl and before dawn came they had to bury the pianist beside the girls. After this gang cleared out, a respectable, hard-working laborer and his family took the place and they had a rough time of it. The mother would make the beds and when she turned to look back in the room as she was leaving, they would be completely mussed up again. She would clean up her kitchen and when she re-entered the room, there would be utter disorder, far worse than what she had just straightened out. The family would sit down to a meal and a cold breeze would send the shivers through each of them, yet no windows or doors were open. And each night the family would hear a piano playing in the house, although neither they nor any neighbors owned such an instrument. The family moved out after a little while, and when new owners took over the property, the bones were found in the cellar. Once they were taken out and buried, the difficulties ceased, and today the place is happily occupied.

The breeze which this family experienced is a fairly common phenomenon. People sometimes describe it as a "strange feeling," or an "unseen presence." People climbing the stairs feel one of these presences as it passes, or a child crawling up, one step at a time, is suddenly given a shove by an unseen hand and sent sprawling to the bottom. Sometimes it is a more specific matter: a hand is felt to drop on the shoulder of one who sits alone by the fire, or someone lying in bed feels a presence sit down beside him. There is no sound, there is nothing to see, but something is there and you know it is there.

The bloodstain that cannot be scrubbed out is something else again. Any man with eyes can see it and anyone who wishes to use a good supply of elbow grease can verify the fact. There is a house in the Helderberg Mountains where a man fell down his cellar stairs, cracking his head open and breaking his neck in one careless movement. Some people said the man was to be seen sometimes coming back with a tool kit to fix the step that caused his death—although a woman who grew up in the place says she never saw him. But the spot of blood on the step would not come out; no matter how much she scrubbed or painted, it always came to the surface. The same thing is true of the house in Constableville where Bill Hinton cut his thoat, and Lord knows how many other places in our parts.

All in all, living in a haunted house can be a nerve-racking experience, what with the noise, the lights, the monkey business with doors and windows, the pulling off of blankets, the moving of furniture, the spooky feelings, and the blood spots that will not be cleansed. Usually there is nothing much anyone can do about it. There are a few rituals that have been tried through the years and that have proved effective. General repairs and the putting in of new doorsills will sometimes do the trick. Some people will tell you that all you really need to do is move the house to a new foundation.

An elderly grandfather sent me word that he really knows how to break the spell of a haunted house; he learned long ago in Germany. First of all you need a certain gift for seeing the returning dead, a gift, fortunately, which he possesses. Then you must stay in the place which is haunted all night by yourself. When you hear or see the ghost, you cross yourself and say, "In the name of the Father, the Son, and the Holy Ghost, who are you and what are you doing here?" Then the ghost will tell you if there is money buried there and where it is. Sometimes he will escort you to the very spot. If he has been murdered and buried there, he will show you the place and then you have to dig up the bones and give them proper burial. Buried money, according to this gentleman, need not be dug up immediately; so long as he has told someone where it is, the ghost who guards it can rest in peace. If you speak to a good ghost, it won't bother you at all, but if you have the misfortune to meet an evil one, a "feeling comes over you that is not pleasant." A bad ghost, according to this authority, will seldom show himself, and if he does, he is usually headless.

There are other methods for eliminating ghosts from a house. The use of holy water, for example, is very common. But the one sure method, which I have seldom heard to fail, is to burn the house down. I know of only one instance in which fire failed to eliminate a ghost. That was up near Sodus where a woman's baby cried and cried one night when there was a bad thunder and lightning storm. Finally the crying drove the mother a little mad, and she stabbed the child to death. After that, whenever there was a thunder and lightning storm you could hear that baby cry, but during one such night the house was struck, and when the fire had finished with it, there was nothing left standing but the fireplace before which the distracted mother had rocked her child the night she had killed it. But even after that, you could still hear the baby's cry on stormy nights, and it was not until the chimney and fireplace were dismantled that you could pass by during a storm and not have the hair rise up along your neck when the shrill, plaintive wail of that baby's ghost pierced the air.

Along with all these other manifestations, the dead occasionally put in an appearance in the houses they haunt. Sometimes this tendency to make themselves visually evident seems no more than the carrying on a lifelong habit; again there is an impish desire for attention; and, naturally, there are those who come back with a set purpose in mind, usually a desire to get some information across the barrier to the living, who, it must be admitted, can be fairly obtuse.

One could name hundreds of examples of those who appear to haunt houses as a matter of habit. Almost any town you might care to name will have at least one such ghost, like the woman in Sag Harbor who still can be seen pacing the widow's walk above her home, waiting for her husband's ship to return from the seas. On Shelter Island there is a house where a whole family has gotten the habit of coming back, a family that has owned their land since Charles II's time. The two old ladies who have lived in the house in recent years are very conscious of their ancestors' presence, and on the whole pleased by it. Outsiders are startled sometimes. One day the maid asked the older sister why she went down to the basement every night to get drinking water when the maid was only too glad to do it for her.

"That isn't I, child, that's my Great-Aunt Sarah."

And there was the time when a niece came to visit with a young doctor she thought it likely she would marry, a very scientific young man who didn't believe in any superstitious nonsense. One morning he was shaving thoughtfully, methodically—almost, one would say, scientifically. Peering intently into the mirror he was suddenly jolted by the sight of another face beside his own. Being a bachelor and used to privacy with his razor, this was a shock. He whirled about, but he had been mistaken; there was no old lady watching him after all. A little more lather, a few more careful strokes, and there was the face again; another fruitless whirling about. It was very annoying; indeed, it was almost disturbing. When he went downstairs he complained about the incident to his hostess. No sooner were the words out of his mouth than he regretted having said anything so absurd. But her answer was, in its own way, reassuring—or would have been to any but a scientific mind.

"Oh, yes," she said, "they come around. We don't have men here very often any more. They're probably pleased."

Late in the night on holidays and family birthdays, the local people say, the two old ladies stand by the head of the stairs and listen to their long-dead relatives holding their parties on the first floor. The silver clatters, the glasses tinkle, and the laughter comes up through the stairwell. No one in that house fears death, for to die means merely that one joins the family at their party in the dining room.

The dead are a persistent lot, and once they get the idea they want the living to learn some fact or do something for them, they keep at it until they are satisfied; if it is necessary to appear repeatedly until they finally get the service they require, why they appear. There is a story of a woman in a little town over in Vermont which is typical. From an empty house weird noises and the shrill cries of a woman were heard repeatedly. Finally half a dozen fellows from the village decided that the only thing to do was to spend the night there and see what they could see. Well, they hung around for hours and just about the time they made up their minds to go on home and get some sleep, they were aware that a woman was in the room, cuddling a baby in her arms. They asked her who she was and what she wanted. She had only one reply to all their questions, and that she repeated, parrotlike:

"He killed me and killed the baby and buried us under the porch."

"He killed me and killed the baby and buried us under the porch."

Then she was gone. Next morning they found what she meant, and after they took the bones to the cemetery, there wasn't any more trouble.

Over and over again the dead return to insure themselves a decent burial in consecrated ground; they object vehemently to being left around in out-of-the-way places. Another thing that worries them is money that they have cached away before they left and that they didn't get around to telling anyone about. If it's in a house they'll stay around it until it is found.

Take that furnished house in South Troy the landlord

could never keep rented because every tenant who took it said it was too scary to live in. There was a man, a tall, thin man with whiskers, who came clumping down from the attic at midnight and went to the parlor where he tapped on the oil paintings with his cane, turned about, and went slowly upstairs again to to disappear until the next night. You couldn't stop him. You could see him, but you couldn't *feel* him; several people had tried. That's what they all said happened; most of them told Sam Barry about it. Sam ran the saloon at Jefferson and First Streets, a few doors away.

Finally, after this had happened five or six times, the landlord hired Sam and five other fellows, at a hundred dollars apiece, to go there and spend the night so as to clear up the matter. The boys sat around and then played some poker. Right on the dot of midnight they heard him coming down the stairs. He did just what the tenants had said he did: walked into the parlor, went to each picture in turn, tapped it with his cane, turned on his heel, and went upstairs again. The boys said afterward that the hair on their heads just stood right up on end. They tried to get their hands on him, but they had no more success than the others. As soon as he had gone back, they locked up and went over to the landlord's house to tell him what they had seen.

They talked the matter over every which way. Finally one of the men asked where the landlord had bought the paintings, for they seemed to be what interested the old man. They had come with the house, along with all the furnishings, which had been bought from the estate of an old fellow of considerable means who had built the house and lived there for years. Maybe they'd better go take a good look at those pictures. Just before dawn they all went back again, the land-lord with them. And behind those oil paintings, inside the frames, and under the wallpaper behind the pictures they found securities and bills worth fifteen thousand dollars. That day they had a priest come in and bless the house, and from then on the old man was content. The living had finally caught on to what he had been trying so clearly to tell them.

There are also ghosts who go to the trouble of re-creating the lost and forgotten past. Not only does one of the dead re-turn to the land of the living but an entire scene, a total mo-ment or way of life is revitalized. And it is this the living see.

Out in Steuben County, for example, a chap took his girl home one evening and started walking to his house. After he had passed several farmhouses he approached a desolate, empty, run-down place generally believed to be haunted. He was grinning to himself about this as he came whistling along. Then he heard music and laughter. The closer he came to the house the louder were the sounds. Then in the moonlight he saw that the old place looked different from the way he had re-membered it: the grass was mowed; the shutters seemed to be straight on their hinges rather than hanging askew; it seemed, in the moonlight, as though the place had a coat of paint on it. When he noticed the light in the windows he decided to go up and take a look to see what was going on there, anyway. Inside, a party was in progress; people were playing cards and dancing. As he watched through the window he was terrified by the high, piercing, agonized scream of a woman, and no sooner had the sound cut the air than the lights went out and he was staring through the broken window of the old de-

serted house he knew. Not wanting to sound like a fool, he
said nothing of his experience for several days to anyone, but
a few nights later when he went to visit his girl again he told
her what he had seen. She seemed not at all surprised, for the
night he told her about was the anniversary of a party which
had taken place in that house many years ago, a party which
had ended in a woman's murder. Each year, at the hour and
instant of the tragedy, they all came back to the house and the
violence was re-enacted.

There is a story told, round about Albany and Troy (and
many other places across the country), which is a kind of folk
classic, ranking with stories of the ghostly hitchhiker which
we shall meet later on. Of several versions, I like it best the
way Sunna Cooper heard it and told it to me.

Fifty years or more ago a man and his wife were traveling
by carriage from somewhere in New England to Troy. They
had passed Eagle Bridge and Johnsonville before they realized that it was getting much too dark for them ever to reach
Troy that night. Just before they reached Spiegletown they
saw a light burning in a little house about three hundred
yards off the main road and, not knowing how near they were
to the village, decided to see if they could get lodgings there
for the night. The man pulled the horse onto the little side
road and climbed the hill to the house. He knocked at the
door. An elderly man and his wife, both of them obviously
ready for bed, came to the door. They were a gentle, kindly
couple, and while they never took paying guests, they would
be delighted to have the travelers spend the night with them.
So the horse was put in the barn while inside the house the

hostess brewed up a pot of tea and brought out some home-
made bread and fresh butter. The four of them chatted a
while before the travelers were taken to their room. It was
then that the man tried to pay for their lodgings, because, he
said, they wished to be on their way early in the morning and
their hosts might not be awake. But the offer was vigorously
refused; they were not in the habit of taking in paying guests
and to pursue the matter would only embarrass them. Leaving it at that, all four went upstairs to bed.

The travelers slept soundly, awakening shortly after sunup.
They dressed quietly and with care, and lest they awaken the
people who had been so kind to them the night before, they
stole downstairs. On a table by the door they placed a fifty-
cent piece, which, fifty years ago, was a fair price for their
lodgings. They got the horse out of the barn, harnessed it,
and drove on to Spiegletown where they had some breakfast.

It was at breakfast that they received their first shock. They
were talking to the man who ran the little restaurant where
they ate and mentioned the very warmhearted reception they
had been given the night before. Just where was this house,
he wanted to know. They told him in great detail and watched
the strange look which came over his face as they did so.

"But, my good friends, I know the house you mean. A family named Brownley lived there for years."

"That's right. That's the name they gave us."

"But—but—that can't be. Both Mr. and Mrs. Brownley
died in the flames three years ago when that house burned to
the ground."

Then there was a great argument, while each side doubted
the other's sanity. Finally there seemed to be only one way to

settle it. The three of them piled into the carriage and drove back the two or three miles to the place where the couple had turned off the road. The horse climbed the little hill, up the three hundred yards to the same spot where they had gone the night before. But there was, in good truth, no house. There was only the gutted cellar, overgrown with weeds and filled with the burned debris. They stood looking at it for a few minutes when all of a sudden the woman screamed and fainted. There in the rubble was a charred and partially burned hall table with a fifty-cent piece on it.

Some people have the knack of getting along with the dead, others go all to pieces. The most successful ones, it seems to me, are blessed with the gifts of courage and serenity. They take the restless dead in the same stride that they take the living. In the stories families bring with them from Italy it is courage which is stressed, sometimes to the great advantage of the living.

Take for example the Damino family, who lived for generations in Castiglione, Italy, before they came to this country. The family was made up of a thriving brood of youngsters, a hard-working, gentle-hearted father, and a mother who was as wise as she was kind and laughter-loving. They moved one time into a big sprawling house which the neighbors assured them was haunted, and they soon believed it. They would come downstairs in the morning and find all the dishes laid out on the floor. At other times it would be the furniture huddled into a corner. Mamma would laugh and say it must have been an earthquake. Then one night they were awakened by the crying of their five-month-old baby, whom they found lying in the middle of the floor, and no one knew how he could have gotten there. This was too much for Mr. Damino: "Let's move. Too many strange things happen in this house." But his wife merely laughed and felt the baby all over to be sure it was unharmed. "No," she said, "we have been lucky in this house. You have prospered and the children keep well. These ghosts will not harm us, if we are not afraid of them, and I am not afraid. We shall stay." And they did stay, with the result that soon the dead left them to their own devices.

Teresa Rossomondo was a woman cut from the same cloth as Mrs. Damino. She was practical and fearless, and blessed with a clear conscience. Twice the dead came to her, but she faced them as imperturbably as she did the living. The first time it was old Sabato Malona who, until he was murdered, had owned the house where the Rossomondos lived in Italy. Everyone said that he was drifting about the house, waiting for his time to be fulfilled, but Teresa knew that the old man had no quarrel with her or hers, so she was not afraid. One night, after a long, laborious day in the fields and in the house, she went to bed early. In her early sleep she thought she heard scuffling and dragging footsteps in the attic, but when someone tugged at her feet she sat up with no sleep in her. There was the old man, spry and mean-faced as ever. The voice was high and cracked that asked, "Teresina, what are you doing in my bed?" Before she could answer him suitably the chimes of midnight rang from the church tower and the old man was gone, and he never came again. (Our American ghosts usually ignore this curfew but not Italian ones.) Another time when she had gone to pick fruit in the orchard of the dead Stanislaura, who had been kind to her when she was a child, he came and touched her on the shoulder. They spoke of the weather and friends, of the harvest and the times. As they stood there she stooped over to place her basket on the ground in order to rest her tired arms, meaning to ask him what brought him back to the old place. When she stood up he was gone, but afterward her only regret was that he never came back; he had been a good friend and it was nice to see him again.

Good fortune came to another Italian woman because she had what Chaucer called "gentil herte." She was married to a man who had grown tired of her. He didn't want to harm her, and he wasn't yearning after anyone else, but he was just tired of the wife that he had. One day he suggested that they move to a little house in the woods, so she gathered up some food and clothes and in a short time was ready to join him. They tried living away from those they knew for a spell, but he was still bored. He decided to leave her. It was very simple: he told her he was going away for a time. Since she was well brought up and an obedient wife she didn't question his going but set herself to getting along in the house alone.

Soon she heard people crying upstairs in an unused part of the house. She went to the bedroom on the second floor where she found a coffin, a corpse, and a group of mourners, weeping and moaning. Her first act was to kneel and pray for the dead man's soul, and then, out of the sympathy in her heart, she wept. Thinking the others would be hungry, she arose from her knees and went downstairs to prepare food for them all. She piled the food on a great tray and trudged up with it to find, when she got back in the room, that corpse and mourners alike had disappeared. The coffin was there, however, filled high with gold. She understood then what had happened. The dead man had needed just one living person to mourn his passing, and when she had prayed and wept she had fulfilled that need. All the people had been wraiths, but the gold was hard and real between her fingers. A day later her husband came that way to see how she was making out. She waved to him to come out of the woods, and when he saw what had come to her he saw her, as it were, in a fresh light. They tell me that it was some time before he tired of her again.

One of my favorite historic houses in this country is Forty Acres in Hadley, Massachusetts. The Porter-Phelps-Huntington family that has lived there for two hundred years has gotten along with their restless ancestress, Elizabeth Porter Phelps, by the simple device of accepting her and her comings and goings and teaching their children to do the same. First a word about the house: it is long and rambling and filled with all the things that other families threw away, generations ago. Never very rich, never very poor, the family had good taste but dwelt in comfort rather than elegance. The house conveys a quality of serenity which one suspects may have been its abiding spirit.

My good friend Dr. James Huntington retired some years ago from practicing medicine to devote himself to preserving and interpreting this house he loves. Elizabeth Phelps is his great-great-grandmother and he loves her too. He has known her all his life, for when he was a boy, on summer nights he would see the little old lady dressed in outdated clothes leaning over his bed. His brothers also saw her on many occasions. The older members of the family took these appear-

ances as a matter of course. "Don't mind that," they would say. "That's only Elizabeth. We've all seen *her*."

The tradition is that Mrs. Phelps was devoted to her son Charles and wanted him to bring his family to the old house to live. It was for this that she had the third-floor attic added. Charles never came and the attic was never finished, but in the dark of the night she goes up to see how it's coming along and to tuck in any young ones who may be sleeping there.

There are no longer children in the house, but Elizabeth is still there. Sometimes an unsuspecting guest turns around to see what might be the source of the rustling sound behind him. Elizabeth wants to know who's there, that's all. Or a small shadow may fall across the floor and a cool breeze pass through the room at the same time. The good doctor always knows what that means. Or coming down the stairs one senses her presence, waiting for the living to pass. Gentle, inquisitive, friendly, she is easy to get along with, but the members of the family have been making it easy for her ever since the end of the Civil War when she first returned, a half century after her death.

I recommend that you go to Hadley, see Forty Acres, see Dr. Huntington, and, if you're lucky, see Elizabeth. Even if you miss her, you will have seen one of our most charming haunted houses.

Chapter Four

Violence and Sudden Death

Those who die violently are the most likely to be foot-loose after death—those drowned at sea, killed in railroad, auto-mobile, and industrial accidents, killed in battle, and most especially those who are murdered or commit suicide. There is a fatalistic logic which assumes that to each of us there is an allotted span and that one whose thread is cut short before his predestined time may spend it wandering the earth. Belief that those who have been murdered and those who die of their own hand come back is probably as old as our civilization. In earlier times the ghost of one murdered, like Hamlet's father, stayed on the scene until his death had been avenged. Into the grave of the suicide was pounded an oaken stake to keep the spirit in its place.

Murder victims are especially prone to haunt their old stamping grounds and pack peddlers were always likely candidates, so that our part of the country has many an isolated farmhouse or woods road with its peddler ghost. The peddler was a man alone, with little contact with people who knew him intimately. His customers were often many miles apart, his itinerary was usually known only to himself, he was defenseless against any numbers, and his pack of desirable articles and the money he had to carry on his person supplied motives. His custom of asking for a place to sleep wherever he found himself must frequently have led him to sleep in the homes of the least desirable of our citizenry. After he had been stabbed quietly in his sleep (often his bloodstains refused to come off the floor), he was dragged down to the cellar and buried in the dirt floor; or instead he was thrown down an abandoned well, or laid to an uneasy rest behind the barn where the woodpile could be stacked over his body. Then the trouble began, for these peddlers were rugged souls who might be murdered in their sleep, but that didn't mean there was the end of it. They came back—as strange lights, as the makers of weird sounds, as the industrious haunters of houses, as wraiths, and in their natural persons. Sometimes they returned regularly, sometimes at annual intervals, sometimes now and then, but they kept coming until their bones were found. Sometimes beside the bones were a few pieces of rusted tinware which their murderers had thought it unwise to keep above ground.

Of course, peddlers aren't the only murder victims to come back. Two or three others will do for now.

One which interests me, because I am a great admirer of the house in which the murder took place, is the ghost who walks along the terrace of the beautiful old colonial mansion known as Cherry Hill, far out on South Pearl Street in Albany.

I had heard as a boy that Cherry Hill was haunted but had forgotten about it until I had a report from one of my friends that neighborhood people had been seeing the murdered man or the murderer again; some said it was one of the Van Rensselaers. When you really want the facts of Albany's past you ask the booksellers. Frank Scopes just snorted when I asked for a verification of my friend's report. Of course, he didn't want to be dogmatic about it, but his recollection was that the murder took place on May 7, 1827, that the man who was killed was young Abraham Van Rensselaer's manager, a fellow named John Whipple, and that the murderer was Mrs. Whipple's lover, a good-for-nothing named Jesse Strang. And somewhere, said Mr. Scopes, he'd seen a pamphlet about the case; if he ever ran across it, he'd let me know. The next time I walked down Maiden Lane he crooked his finger at me, and there was the pamphlet, located under Lord knows how high a mountain of books.

As murders go, it wasn't a very interesting one and undoubtedly much of its contemporary interest derived from both of the principals being employees of the Van Rensselaer family. John Whipple was, as Frank Scopes said (I have yet to catch him in a factual error), the manager of young Van Rensselaer's estate at Cherry Hill. This was a position of considerable responsibility because Abraham Van Rensselaer was barely of age, his father having died but a year or so before the murder. There had come to work around the place but recently this chap named Jesse Strang, who soon developed a friendship for Mrs. Whipple. They spent a truant weekend together and a few days later he bought a revolver. On the night of May 7 he learned that his mistress's husband was in a back room on the second floor of the main house, going over accounts with his employer. Strang climbed up on a roof outside the window and shot through the glass, killing Whipple instantly. He was quickly taken, and the trial, a three-day wonder, sent him to the gallows and Mrs. Whipple to the penitentiary. When they hanged him, spectators drove from as far away as Cooperstown to see the spectacle.

But now comes the problem: *who* is the ghost? Assuming, and I think it is a safe assumption, that it is one of the principals, which one? Is it Strang, pacing up and down, as he may have done before he collected the courage to shoot his mistress's husband? Is he waiting for some rendezvous with her? It could be, of course, but it is unlikely, for almost never does the murderer posthumously return to the scene of the crime; almost invariably it is the victim who comes back. (There is one exception: when the murder is re-enacted and both murderer and murdered reappear.) So, the chances are that it is Whipple, waiting for something, maybe for Strang, maybe for his wife—maybe he is still on the job keeping a weather eye on Cherry Hill, a stately island out of the past surrounded by the rushing tide of the industrial present.

The Hudson River has three tributaries named for some murderer. There is the Moordenerskill (Dutch for Murderer's Creek) in Rensselaer County, the Moodna Kill (apparently another form of the same) just south of Newburgh, and Murderer's Creek in Greene County. The ghost of the woman whose death gave the Greene County stream its name has been known to return. On one occasion the Woman in White climbed right up on a wagon and took a ride with the poor terror-stricken driver. Her name, according to another source, was Mary Johnson, and she had been murdered by a George Eliot in 1841. They buried her under the bridge and for years she appeared there and on occasion even kept good Episcopalians from crossing the bridge on their way to church in the Upper Village.

In the same stream there is an island named for Sally Hamilton who met violent death farther downstream, but when the tide came in her body was floated up to the island and discovered there. Sam Frisbee saw her more than once and told Clarice Weeks about it.

"When I came back home there was some trouble, so I went to this boardinghouse to live. The house was halfway down the hill into the Brick Row. . . . A man named Dave Bush slept with me in the southeast room upstairs—that corner room."

"How long ago was this?" Clarice wanted to know.

"Thirty-five years ago, mebbe more. Well, we had heard

about people seeing things in this house before, but as I say, I've never been afraid of anything—much less ghosts.

"This one night it was rather cool and I woke up about midnight and found I had no covers.

" 'Dave, give me some covers.'

" 'No, I won't,' he answered. 'I won't because I can't. I ain't got any.'

"So I got up and lit one of those big old kerosene lamps. I looked all around and there, in front of the door, rolled up and pushed right against the closed door, was our blankets. I brought the covers back to bed but I lay there wonderin' who could have done it and gotten out of the room. Then, for a few nights nothing happened.

"One night we came back from downstreet—I guess it was the first time they had movies in Jerry Brooks' Opery House. About midnight Dave poked me. 'S-S-Sam! S-S-Sam! There it is! Look!'

" 'You're dreaming, Dave. Wake up.'

" 'I'm not dreaming. I'm awake. Look against the door.'

"Sure enough, there she was, a beautiful female figure. Looked at first as if she might have a wedding dress on. I couldn't see her face clear, because she was sort of pale and faint—right there in front of our closed door. But it wasn't a wedding dress, I was sure of that later on.

"I wasn't afraid, so I got out of bed and walked across the room to investigate. All the while I kept my eye on her. Then I grabbed for her with both hands. There was nothin' there!

"I thought that someone might be playing a joke on us. Then I thought maybe it was the reflection of lights in Hudson on the windows or something like that. But when I got back in bed she was still gone. Let me tell you, it was a funny feeling. I wasn't scared; I've *never* been scared, but it did give me a funny feeling."

Clarice suggested it might have been the bride who disappeared from that house when her bridegroom was killed a few hours after their wedding. But Sam was sure it wasn't the bride.

"There used to be a beautiful girl from downstreet named Sally Hamilton—that's who it was. She used to visit at that house where I was. I knew her, such a beautiful girl! She used to wear a lot of jewelry—pins, rings, necklaces, and all that. She used to walk up the lower road to Herr's Camp and over a short cut to the Spoorenburg Road that we called Korst Veloren Road—that's Low Dutch, you know. Some fellow murdered her and her body floated up Murderer's Creek to a little island, but there wasn't any jewelry on her body when they found her. Some folks said a deserter from the army did it. No one knows. No one knows. But that's what I saw, anyway."

The dead choose strange ways to make themselves manifest, and this is true in Italy as elsewhere. To understand this next tale it is necessary to know about a belief held in the section of northern Italy around Barre that if one is murdered without cause, his spirit leaves his body to enter the nearest urn of water. The first person to drink from the urn swallows the spirit. This sometimes causes him to turn into a snake or to do strange and unaccountable deeds. The young girl Angelica did not turn into a snake after the murder of

Pietro took place a short distance from her home, but she did undergo a definite change. She had been a normal, willowy girl who enjoyed the life of the village and took little thought of tomorrow. Pietro was murdered in the evening, and she heard his screams but did not realize at the time what was happening. In the morning she was the first member of her household to be up and around, and so first drank from the urn of cool water they kept by the door. Apparently Pietro's spirit was in the water, for her stomach began to bloat and she began to say queer things. She could foretell the future: who would marry, who would be unfortunate, who stole, and where the stolen goods were hidden. When they asked her what had brought about this change in her, she could only shake her head, as though she herself did not know the reason, though everyone else was satisfied that it was Pietro who spoke to them through her. Always just before she was able to speak of the future she would make a peculiar sound and her stomach would swell up. Angelica lived to be twenty-two, and three days before her death one of her patron saints came to her in a vision and told her to prepare herself. The day she was to die she dressed in her best clothes and lay down upon her bed to await the death that came before the sun set.

Mrs. Rose Malerba, the woman who told the story of Angelica, was in those days a girl herself in Barre, engaged to marry a successful young lawyer. Angelica told her on one occasion that within a few months she would discover that her fiancé was being unfaithful to her and that their engagement would be broken. She would then go to America where she would meet a man from a neighboring village and after a short courtship marry him. At the time the whole prophecy sounded fantastic, but as she tells of it now in Albany it seems stranger yet, for that is exactly the way her life worked out.

If Angelica's spirit is typically Old World, the second shooting of "Red" Halloran is in the American thriller tradition.

Some years ago in Chicago there was a tough gang leader named Red Halloran who bought himself, at the height of his power, a magnificent, custom-built, bulletproof, sixteen-cylinder dream car. It had everything, with a few extras added. Then came a day when he had to make a quick getaway. He roared out of Chicago all by himself and ran spang into a police ambush; bulletproof car or no, they filled him full of lead.

Just how the car got to New York or how it acquired a reputation for being haunted, I do not know, but when the dealers tried to hire someone to drive it to California to its new owner, its reputation was well enough established so that no one wanted to take the job. Finally they found a newspaper reporter who had just been fired and who agreed to take it west for a hundred dollars and expenses. The boys at the garage told him he'd never get it past Chicago, but he'd heard stories like that before.

The early part of his trip was entirely uneventful. He had decided to sleep in the car and thus to pocket the money he had been allowed for lodgings. Somewhere in Illinois he began to get sleepy again, so he drove the car onto a side road and curled up to take a few winks. When he awoke the car was being driven very rapidly by a man he had never seen before, a burly redheaded character who would answer neither his questions nor his protestations, a character who kept on whistling "Yankee Doodle" and driving the car as though the Devil himself were following.

After a few uncomfortable miles the reporter noticed police patrol cars up ahead; the driver noticed them too and went past them like a bat out of Hell, completely ignoring their signals to stop. With that, the police began to shoot, and the driver made a desperate effort to pull around a patrol car they had parked across the middle of the road. In that fleeting second the reporter made two moves: he grabbed the wheel with one hand and turned off the ignition with the other. It was then he realized that the driver had disappeared and he was sitting there in the front seat by himself.

When he tried to tell the police what had happened, he fully expected them to call him a liar, but several of them had seen the redheaded driver. And others recalled the curious fact that on that very spot and under identical circumstances Red Halloran had been killed. And when they heard the reporter's description of his driver, they knew all too well why he was not in the car when they got to it. So they let the reporter go on his way while they went back to waiting for a stolen car they had been looking for in the first place.

There is a story they tell in the Adirondacks which recalls the ancient belief that a ghost of one who has been murdered stays on earth until he has been avenged, a belief which seems to be generally rejected in our time.

Two men had a hunting camp, not far from St. Regis Falls in the North Woods. Every season they would go up there for a few days' hunting, just the two of them. Everybody assumed they were good friends until one day a few years ago when one of the men—we'll call him Conklin, because that wasn't his name—came down out of the woods alone. Conklin said his friend Barry had got lost, and so a search party went back up in the woods with him, but just then the snow set in and they didn't find any trace of the missing man.

The State Police thought there was something fishy about the whole business. Conklin got flustered when they asked him too many questions, and anybody could see that he wasn't telling the whole story. But they didn't have any evidence, and moreover they didn't have any corpse to prove murder, so the case was dismissed.

In the spring Barry was found lying at the base of a tree with his skull broken. Still the police couldn't prove anything, and when the coroner's jury turned in a verdict it was "from accidental death, cause or causes unknown," or whatever it is they say in cases like that. Beside his body they had found his rifle, all rusty now, but his hunting knife was missing from the case on his leg where he carried it. Nobody thought much of that at the time.

The next fall Conklin went back to his camp with a new companion. The first night they were there, the newcomer turned in early. It had been a long trip and he had fallen into a very deep sleep when he was jolted awake by Conklin, who was screaming, "Don't do it! Don't do it!" He pulled himself out of the bunk and found his flashlight. There was Conklin dead in his chair, with a hunting knife stuck in his heart. A curious detail was the discovery of the fingerprint expert when they took the knife to police headquarters.

There was only one set of prints on the handle of the knife and those were quite clear: they belonged to Barry.

Another story of ghostly revenge doesn't involve a murder —at least not at first—but it does involve a couple of other interesting bad habits. This version comes from an Italian family, but my wife says that as a girl in New York City she heard a version of it from a German playmate.

It began when a rather surly and overbearing husband brought home a pound of calf's liver. It was midday, and since the noon meal was waiting to be eaten, he told his wife to cook the meat for supper. She had brought the food out under the arbor, and they sat there together in an unusually pleasant mood, for he was not what one would call an amiable man. She told him how the body of the rich, old gentlewoman of the village who had died the day before had been brought to the church next door. The man was not particularly interested in her prattle, but his mouth was full of good ravioli which he kept washing down with equally good Chianti, and he did not want to stop eating long enough to tell her to be quiet. Besides, it probably did little harm to permit a woman to talk now and then, so long as she did not pretend that what she said mattered. Finally he said, "Enough," and his wife, not knowing whether he referred to his meal or her conversation, became silent. After dozing in his chair for a spell he went back to his shop, and a lazy afternoon drifted into eventide.

As the time for his return approached, his woman began the preparation and the slow, well-seasoned cooking which liver properly requires. After a while she lifted the lid and peeked at the meat. It looked done, but to be sure she cut a little piece from the edge and popped it into her mouth. It was good; the flour had formed a delicious crispness around the edge, and the flavor was rich and right. She tried another piece, and another, and another. She was ravenous and she had no power to stop herself until the pan was empty. Then she remembered her husband and panic shook her. He was not a man to whom one could explain that the meat he had brought home at noon had tasted so good that there was none for his dinner. Too often she had felt the beatings he dealt her when the world went contrary to his plans. It was then she thought of the rich widow lying alone before the altar.

It was a fine meal, and the man rose from his table well satisfied with the world. It had been a good day; customers had kept him busy at his shop, the noon meal had been pleasant, and now he'd had a dinner fit for the gods, green salad with rich olive-oil dressing touched by just the right amount of garlic and vinegar, fresh bread, and the tenderest, tastiest liver that ever a man set to his lips. He looked his woman over, seeing her with new eyes. She had a variety of uses— all of them, he chuckled to himself, satisfactory. "It is time," he said, "for us to go to bed."

Perhaps he had drifted off to sleep before it happened, though his wife had not yet closed her eyes. It was a voice, close to their ears, yet from a distance: "My liver! I want my liver! Give me my liver!" It was the voice of a woman, an old and cultured woman. The cry came again and again, piercing and terrible. "My liver, give me back my liver!" At last the wife could stand the strain no longer, and in a tumbling flood of confession she spilled out the story.

As she told it, he could almost see her slit the belly of the widow's corpse, thrust in her long-fingered hand until she found the organ she was seeking, deftly cut it out, rearrange the clothes, and speed out of the church, back to her stove and frying pan. It explained her own lack of appetite which he had considered so fortunate at mealtime. As he weighed the matter in his mind, the point which disturbed him was that it was he who had eaten the liver and that undoubtedly it would be upon him that the dead woman would wreak her vengeance. He had some idea of the kind of havoc a really aroused ghost could bring about.

Both women had ceased speaking now, though the living

one at his side lay moaning softly into her pillow. There was only one thing a man could do, he decided, under the circumstances. He got out of bed and went into the kitchen, coming back with the carving knife. Fortunately his wife fainted before he drew the fine sharp blade along her sleek belly. A few minutes later he stole into the church to give the old woman a new liver to replace the one he had eaten. One wonders whether he did not look upon the meat just a bit longingly, for the corpse was getting a much better organ than she had lost. At any rate, the old girl was satisfied and never disturbed his sleep in the nights that followed.

A special group of ghosts consists of persons murdered specifically to guard treasure buried with them. Not all haunted treasure is protected by a murder victim, but some is. In my part of America, haunted treasure was usually buried by pirates, by Indians, by settlers during the French and Indian Wars, by Tories during the Revolution, or by latter-day misers who had no faith in banks and a strong sense that the earth was the place for man's valuables. Murder was committed so that a ghostly guardian might serve the owner of the treasure, for if a young person were placed in the hole with the treasure, he would be there to guard it for what would have been his normal span of life—presumably a longer span than the life expectancy of the owner. One other characteristic of haunted treasure in our area is this: it is almost never found by those who search for it.

All through the nineteenth century there were stories current along the Hudson Valley that Captain Kidd had buried his treasure there, and many a time the moon looked down on men digging hopefully for it.

Close to a hundred years ago, in the town of Hughsonville between Beacon and Poughkeepsie, a woman named Talmage had a dream. She was an old woman then, tall, with full lips, an aquiline nose, and cold blue eyes. She had been born on Hallowe'en just before midnight, and she had been born with a caul. When she told fortunes with tea leaves her eyes were like blue crystals which held all the secrets of the past and the future. This woman dreamed the same dream on three successive nights when she was ninety years old.

In this dream she saw a tall man, whom she recognized as Captain Kidd, burying gold at the base of a giant oak in a grove of trees not four miles from where she was sleeping. She could see the gold pieces plainly enough to describe them exactly the following morning. The next night, and the next, the dream was repeated, each time identical with that of the preceding night, each time most specifically clear. The repetition and the clarity, and perhaps some urging from the lady herself, caused the men in her family to plan a little action.

Matt Talmage and his brother Jim set out for the grove one night shortly after the third dream. In the back of the buckboard they carried a bull's-eye lantern, two shovels, a pick, and a potato sack. Just before they started, Matt slid a rifle in with the other things. There were a number of reasons for going at night: there was farm work in the daytime; they had no wish either to be followed or to be laughed at; but most especially, the old lady had told them to go at night, and she had a way of speaking that forestalled contradiction and disobedience. She had told them to go at night and to say no

word to each other once they got there, for silence is the required rule when it comes to digging haunted treasure. Absolute silence.

The moon was shining when they started out, but the
woods were very dark and when they came to the grove it
was pitch-black. They lit the bull's-eye lantern and quickly
found the giant tree of which the old lady had spoken. It was
easily found, for it dominated the entire grove. They were
silent now, pointing to the spot they had been told to find, the
place "between the folds of the tree that formed two huge
roots." They were scared: the owls made the only sounds and
the silent bats swooped low over their heads; not even a star
could be seen through the heavy roof of foliage.

Jim had begun the digging, and after twenty minutes' work
he was tired, but the pile of dirt beside the tree was beginning
to grow. He looked up to Matt to ask him to take over, but
his eyes went beyond his brother and by the reflected light of
the bull's-eye lantern Matt saw Jim's mouth gape open and a
look of terror come over his face. Matt felt his own blood go
icy and his neck and spine tingle with panic. Then he turned
around and looked.

There, standing with his elbow level with the seat of their
high wagon, was a man, ten feet or more in height. That it
was the same man the old lady had described to them was beyond all doubt. Slowly a great arm rose and with an imperious
gesture motioned them to leave the grove. For a few seconds
they were frozen to the spot where they stood, but as the giant
started to walk toward them they found their feet. Matt
screamed and they both started running. They circled the
figure, clambered onto the wagon, and tore out of the grove

toward home. They whipped the horse, but it was hardly necessary, for he seemed to share their panic.

The next morning, after very little sleep, Matt and Jim went back to the grove. Even in the morning light the grove was dark and the shadows of their fears from the previous night were in the air. There by the giant oak lay their tools, just where they had left them the night before. But the ground between the great spreading roots was as though it had not been touched for centuries. Each particle of moss was in its place; even the ant hills were undisturbed. Yet there was no question but that it was the place where Jim had piled high a heap of dirt the night before. There was no way of proving it now, and the two brothers looked at each other speechlessly. They gathered up their tools and went home.

That night they told what had happened in the local tavern and took a good deal of ribbing for it. But after the tavern was shut for the night, a little group collected some tools and hitched up a wagon and went to the grove to find out for themselves. They found out. It happened to them just as it had happened to Jim and Matt. The mountain of a man had spoken no words but they could no more have stayed there than they could have lifted themselves on wings.

When Matt and Jim told the old lady what had happened to them, she was not surprised. "The man who gets the treasure must outwit him, that's all."

Well, as I hear it, every decade or so, somebody tries it. Thirty years ago three boys from Brockway set out at ten o'clock one night to get those gold pieces. They left the Gold Coast Cafe in an old Model T. The car was found next day in the road near the grove, but the boys haven't been seen or heard from since. But the tree is still there in the grove, towering over it like an old pirate captain bullying his crew from the bridge.

While this is a fairly typical example of the problems facing the hunters of haunted treasure, there are some variations of which one should be forewarned. Sometimes the spirit which guards the treasure is headless, sometimes it is in the shape of a dog. Sometimes counter charms are used to keep the treasure from disappearing when it is located. One man out in LeRoy used a long rod with the letters G O D stamped on it. The sharp points of the two ends were tipped with silver. Once the box was found, it was to be pierced by the rod and that would hold it in place so that it wouldn't disappear. The only trouble with that invention was that the owner never got near enough to pierce the box, much less to keep it from disappearing. The experience of Matt and Jim of having the ground seemingly untouched when they went back to investigate the next morning is a commonplace among treasure hunters. Not infrequently they inadvertently break the taboo against speaking, and no sooner have the words fallen from their lips than the treasure sinks out of sight and the dirt falls into the hole; the sod rolls back into place, and there is nothing to do but go on home and forget about it.

From the Helderberg Mountains west of Albany comes a complicated ritual to insure the finding of treasure, although I know of no one who claims that he has found any this way. Nor have I used it myself, so you may take it for what it is worth. First of all you must locate a spot that seems mysterious and a likely spot for the treasure to be hidden. You go there at midnight without light of any sort, and remember not to say a word all the while you are there. First you dig a hole; then you take some of the dirt from the hole and cover over a sheep buck. You place a turkey gobbler on top of the dirt over the sheep buck, and then you cover that with dirt from the same hole. Then you place a rooster on top of the pile and cover him over with more of the dirt. By this time you have a good-sized pile, and that is all you can do for that first night.

If you can continue to maintain silence during the second night you are certain of your treasure. First you uncover the rooster, who will jump up and fight you. You must kill the rooster and then uncover the gobbler. He will fight you too, but you must kill him, maintaining perfect silence all the time. Then you take care of the sheep buck in the same way, and if you can do him in silently, then you can start digging, and if there is treasure there, you will find it.

This has the earmarks of being a fragment of a European tale which has been lost in the New York hills. It calls to mind a story told by an Italian family living in Schenectady.

Early one morning a poor fisherman was on his way to his boat when a young boy called to him from beside the road.

"Come here," said the boy.

"I can't," said the fisherman. "I have to catch fish so my family can eat."

"Would you like to be rich?"

The fisherman went over to the boy to see what all this was about. The boy told him that some robbers had asked him to guard some treasure for them and then had killed him. Now the fisherman could have gold and jewels beyond price, if he would do just as the boy directed.

"Go into the cave there beyond that tree. I'll be right behind you. First you will meet a snake. Don't be afraid; just step over the snake and keep walking. Then you'll come to two snarling dogs. Don't be afraid; I'll be right behind you. Finally you will see a man with a shotgun sitting on the treasure. He'll say, 'Don't move or I'll shoot.' When he says that, fall right on the treasure and touch it. It will be yours, if you do just as I say."

"All right," said the fisherman, "let's go."

The two entered the cave and came upon the snake. The boy said, "Go on. I'm right behind you. Don't look back for me, but I'll be here all the time."

The two dogs looked frightening, but the voice of the boy reassured him and he stepped over the dogs. He went on till he came to the man with the shotgun.

"Don't move or I'll shoot," warned the man.

The poor fisherman was paralyzed with fright. He turned around and cried, "I can't do this. I can't leave my family."

That did it! Everything disappeared. He found himself out in a field all by himself. Soon the boy appeared, angry and disappointed. He told the fisherman that if his instructions had been carried out the man would have been rich and the boy's soul could have gone to rest. Now someone else would have to be found. He cursed the man, saying that he always would be poor and always wear rags.

A few days later the man bought a new pair of overalls and the first time he wore them he tore a big hole in the knee. He was ragged and poverty-stricken as long as he lived.

The little boy in that story recalls the attractive ghost called Mazzo Maoriello told of by people in Amsterdam, New

York, from Rome, Italy. He was a little boy all dressed in white and wearing a saucy red cap. Mazzo had finished his task of guarding somebody's gold for the full period of what would have been his normal lifetime, and yet he stayed in this world. He liked to join the other children in play, and grownups would find him happily romping with their young and invite him into their homes for dinner. Everyone knew that he was from the other world, but no one was afraid of him and everybody hoped that sometime he would reveal where the treasure which he had been forced to guard lay buried. If he still remembered, he never told. But when folks came to move from one home to another he was likely to be on hand to help, for there was something about the ritual of moving that appealed to him; perhaps he was stirred by some memory from the long ago when he was a real child and shared the excitement that comes to every family when it changes houses.

I don't want to leave the impression that only children, giants, and monsters guard haunted treasure, or that it is always done in a malevolent spirit. Sometimes the owner seems merely to be watching out to see that the right sort eventually comes into possession of his gold.

There was a haunted house in Trenton, New Jersey, that no tenant would stay in very long because of the ruckus a ghost made all the time. After a while a woman who had lived a mighty careless sort of life went to the landlord and told him that she wasn't afraid of any ghost that walked. He said, "All right, if you're sure you won t be afraid."

She'd been there a few nights when she had occasion to go

down in the cellar. At the foot of the stairs this great dark thing rose up in front of her. "What the hell do you want?" she asked. All she remembered after that was falling; when they found her next day every hair of her head had been burned right off. She got out of there as fast as she could get.

The next tenant was a good church woman who sewed every Tuesday for the missionary society and who went to prayer meetings on Wednesday nights. The landlord explained the situation to her before she moved in. "Don't you worry," she said. "I'll stay."

A few nights after she arrived she wanted something down in the cellar too, so she lit a candle and went down the stairs. This same "thing" rose up in front of her. "Good friend, what in the name of God is it that you want? Is there anything troubling you that it is in my power to help?" This "thing," this ghost, motioned to her to follow him, and they went over to a corner of the cellar. Then he pointed for her to put down her candle. As she did this she noticed a loose block of cement in the floor that she had never observed before. She lifted it out and there she found a neat box set in the floor, filled with gold pieces. She was flabbergasted. "Is this for me?" she asked the ghost, but when she turned to look for him he was gone, and as they tell it in Trenton, he hasn't returned since.

I have never seen statistics analyzing the relative popularity of different methods of committing suicide but there must be such available. I raise the point because such a vast majority of the ghosts whose last mortal act was self-destruction seem to have preferred hanging to the other possibilities. The very ropes they hang themselves with become haunted—like the one in a Pine Plains barn that appeared every time anyone entered there. They had cut a man down from the rafters in 1845, but the rope kept reappearing. They would cut it down again and again, but there it was the next time they walked into the barn. And there is that bell rope in Katsbaan: one wintry midnight some years ago the good folk of the community heard the bell ring and a few hardy souls got dressed and trudged over to the church to see what mischief-maker or what catastrophe could be the cause. A stranger's body was swinging back and forth, with the bell rope about his neck. Who he was or why he chose the Katsbaan bell rope as his method of departure was never known, but some say that if you are awake in the middle of the night on the anniversary of the event you can just hear the clapper as it taps the bell.

Suicides are great ones for haunting houses, as has already been suggested, and they go through all the antics that other ghosts do. I have no reason to believe that the returning suicide is any different from the rest, but sometimes one of them will work out a specialty which separates him from the general run. There is a house in Saugerties in which a man hanged himself in the attic fifty years or more ago. Thereafter it was impossible to keep a candle or a kerosene lamp burning in the attic, and whenever anyone entered it the door would bang shut behind him. Eventually some owner had the place wired for electricity, but even then it was impossible to make a light go on in that part of the house. They tell me that if you were to go up there tonight with a flashlight, it would flicker out.

I have also heard of a woman whose husband was a salesman on the road and one day he came home to find she had done herself in. The next tenants had a terrible time: she would go upstairs and open the bedroom doors and go back down again; she would go to the attic and make noises as though she were moving boxes and cases about, but when they were examined they seemed not to have been moved; she would turn the key in a lock while someone was watching the door, but when the door was opened she was not there. And on two occasions she did something I know of no other ghost doing. She would go over to the telephone and dial it; people in the room could see and hear it happen. No one seems to have had the presence of mind to lift the receiver and find out whom she was calling, and so a good story is lost. Makes you wonder, though, when the telephone bell rings in the middle of the night and you crawl out of bed to answer it, and there is no voice at the other end. At least it makes me wonder.

Two of my favorite ghosts drowned themselves, and each in its own way is unique. We might call them the cases of the persistent fisherman and the girl in the Pink House.

Thirty or thirty-five years ago a family named Johnson moved into the valley of the Kuyahoora, which branches off from the Mohawk at Herkimer. They bought a little old stone farmhouse on one of the Norway–Middleville roads. The house had been neglected and empty for several years previous to their coming. The neighbors predicted that they wouldn't stay long; nobody ever did because the place was badly haunted, but the Johnsons were not to be driven out of their new home by silly gossip and superstitious foolishness.

But it wasn't as easy as that. Under the stairway leading up from the front hall, there was a tiny closet the door of which was secured by a wooden turn-knob. Each morning Mary Johnson found that little door wide open, and each morning she closed it again, only to find it open again the following morning. That sort of experience starts out by being annoying, then it becomes an irritation, and after that it becomes a nightmare. They put a chain on the door, but that didn't work, because just before dawn the chain rattled so loudly that everyone in the house was awakened out of a sound sleep. Between chain rattling and an opened door, the Johnsons chose to take the chain off and throw it away.

At just about this point in the story Mary Johnson's brother John came for a visit. He was a great fisherman, and since there was a fine trout stream nearby, he decided to get up before the rest of the family one morning and see what he could catch for breakfast. He took his rod and went to the ruins of an old mill on the banks of a millpond through which the trout stream passed. In the first light of dawn he saw an old man fishing on the banks of the pond. He was an odd-looking duck, wearing an old-fashioned ulster, and he sat with his rod secured in the forked branch of a fallen tree.

"How's the luck?" asked John.

No answer.

"I say, how's the fishing?" this time in a louder voice, but still no answer. Finally, deciding the old man just wanted to be left alone, he walked on downstream, but after a few feet he looked back to discover that the old man had vanished. It didn't make sense; the land thereabouts was flat and there were only a few big trees. The man hadn't had time to walk off. Either he was in the pond or he was in the ruined mill. John peered down into the clear, shallow water and there

was nothing there but some fish which would make a fine treat for breakfast. Then he examined the cavernous interior of the mill and there was nothing there but rotted beams and weeds.

He went back to the place where he had seen the old man, and he was surprised to observe that the soft ground for many yards around showed no footprints but his own. There was no hole in the ground where he had seen the crotched stick. He began to think he was going mad.

Later that day he told his experience to an ancient inhabitant of the community who brightened right up when he heard the description of the vanishing fisherman. There was no question about it, that was old Mr. Brockhurst who lived in the Johnson's house for years. Used to go fishing every morning of the year when it was possible to get at the fish. He had been very particular about his fishing tackle, of which he had a fine assortment. Used to keep it in a little closet under the stair and heaven help the person who tampered with it! Drowned in that same millpond.

The Pink House in Wellsville, ten miles from the Pennsylvania border, is the focal point of a cumulative legend of haunting by a suicide. This is particularly interesting in view of the fact that there is a printed version of the story (in verse) which bears only superficial likeness to the story which is developing among the people of the area.

Most old settlers agree that the story in the poem "Pauline," by Hanford Lennox Gordon, is substantially the correct one. This is a tale told by a dying soldier at Appomattox and concerns a cruel, rich father, a sweet and simple daughter, a poor but honest lover. This father was the builder of the Pink House, the man who first gave it the color it has to this day, a lumber merchant in Wellsville, hard as nails in everything except what touched his daughter. It was in the village school that she, Pauline, met the son of a poor widow who lived on the outskirts of town. The youngsters grew up together, and by the time they reached high school they were in love, although her father knew nothing of this romance. Only once did the boy ever come to the Pink House; that was the day he was to leave the village to study law in the city. They had the misfortune to be caught in each other's arms by the master of the house on that occasion, whereupon Pauline's father called the boy a good many nasty names, among them "beggar," which bitterly hurt his natural pride. Despite these insults the lovers carried on a clandestine correspondence until her father sent each of them a forged letter purporting to come from the other which effectually stopped the letter writing and left each of them hurt and angry. A year or so later, word came to the boy that Pauline was marrying a rich, middle-aged newcomer to the town whom her father had encouraged for financial reasons. The lovers met once more, this time on the streets of Wellsville the day before her wedding. When Pauline and her father passed the boy in their carriage, his attitude was very nonchalant and one who had seen them would have assumed that whatever had passed between the couple was dead.

That night the boy decided that in the morning he would go to the Pink House to ask her forgiveness, but in the morning he was awakened by a friend who came to tell him that Pauline had drowned herself in a fountain at the Pink House.

Then it was that the Pink House began to show signs of being haunted. People would enter the library and have the feeling that a woman had just left it by another door—and there would be Mrs. Browning's *Sonnets from the Portuguese,* opened and turned face down on the sofa. At night they would hear the piano playing pieces which Pauline had enjoyed playing, and at other times the scent of the perfume which she used would be particularly strong in a room, as though she had just left it.

This, then, is the way the story is told in print. We now

turn to the oral tradition as it is growing in the area round about Wellsville.

One tradition says that a man married one of two sisters and came to his wife's home to live; what he did not know until she drowned herself in the millpond on the grounds was that his sister-in-law was also in love with him. In this story there is no ghost. Other versions develop this theme and add to it the tradition of haunting which we have already encountered in the "Pauline" version.

Thirty miles from Wellsville they will tell you that the family had two daughters, the older of whom was engaged to be married and her trousseau was all made, waiting for the important day. Out of a clear sky came the shocking news that her fiancé had eloped with her younger sister. The bride-that-was-to-have-been was so heartbroken that she drowned herself in the swimming pool. After a year or so the sister and her husband came back to live in the Pink House. First, stories began to circulate that the dead sister was seen in the moonlight near the pool. She was seen on the walk to the house; she was seen passing through the door. Then one night the couple was suddenly awakened by something cold and clammy on their faces. The next night they kept their eyes open, and they saw the dead sister enter their room and come beside their bed. Then she threw back her head and with a quick movement she tossed her wet hair across their faces and drew it toward her before she vanished into the shadows forever.

From Professor Thompson's archive at Cornell comes the best telling of this story I have found. I would like to quote it as it was written by Mrs. Edward W. Wilson. Her beginning

is very like the one above and we pick it up after the elopement.

"No letter of explanation from the hasty couple on their
unscheduled honeymoon could temper the grief of the father,
nor the dismay of the jilted girl, who, rather than see her
former lover bring home his new bride, drowned herself in
the marble fountain in front of the Pink House. This double
shock saddened the father, who, nevertheless, forgave his
older daughter and welcomed her back home. A year later, he
had a granddaughter who for two years brought happiness to
the Pink House. Then a strange thing happened; the little
girl began avoiding her parents and wanting to be alone. She
wanted only to toddle about the gardens all by herself, often
rising from her bed at night to wander aimlessly in the moonlight. One night, her aunt appeared and beckoned to the little
girl to follow her down the carpeted staircase, across the en-
trance hall, out into the fateful fountain, where the body of
the poor little innocent was found the next morning. The
relentless spirit of the aunt continued to haunt the Pink
House every night, bringing sleeplessness and worry to all its
occupants. The grief-stricken grandfather now turned against
his older daughter and her husband, sent them away from
Wellsville, and soon followed his granddaughter to the
grave. . . .

"At length the owners of the mansion returned home, now
with another two-year-old daughter, whom they were deter-
mined to watch over night and day. And it is well they did,
for on the night of their home-coming the wraith appeared
before her second niece, beckoning her to follow. The frantic
father, on vigil in the child's room, lit a candle, whereupon

the spectre departed. Each night after that a light was kept burning in the child's room, and only once (when the candle flickered) did the ghost reappear. With candle-light replaced by gas, and then by electricity, an ever-burning light was maintained in the girl's room, where even to-day passers-by may see it, though the niece is nearing eighty, and her parents have left the Pink House forever."

CHAPTER FIVE

Haunted History

A man who set his mind to it could probably write a ghostly history of the United States. It might take a while to garner all the stories the people tell, but certainly we would find representative men and women from every crucial period of our past who have returned. The memories of their comings have been cherished by the people who have told and retold their stories.

Naturally, we begin with the Indians, and as with so much of our lore about the aborigines, the ghost tales frequently

tell more about the sentimental enthusiasms of our nine-
teenth-century forebears than about the Indians themselves.
A case in point is the Indian chief of Conesus Lake. Every
year when the vacationers go out to the lake they delight to
hear the old-timers say their say, and if some visitors are
doubtful, others are open-minded enough to line the shores of
the lake on August evenings, hoping that they may see what
others swear that they have seen. What there is to see comes
when the August moon is full, and something about the night
convinces them that they have seen an Indian chieftain, wearing phosphorescent war paint that glows in the moonlight.
What they enjoy most of all is the legend of the young Indian
wife who could no longer stand the beatings her chieftain
husband gave her and who in desperation ran away with her
warrior lover from another tribe. They made good their
escape, but her husband continued the search for many years.
Eventually he devoted a day's token search to them once a
year, and this much he vowed he would do forever. And he
does.

A happier couple haunt Indian Lake. Once again it was a
chieftain (we don't deal in anything less when we grow sentimental about the savages), one Sabeal, who went out into
the woods about his mountain home and never returned. As
the long wintry hours dragged on, his wife, worried and grief-
stricken, set out over the ice-covered lake to find him. His
body they never located, but hers, frozen stiff, was found a
few days later. They buried her on a little island where, as
dusk settles down you can still hear, if your ears are sharp,
the voice of her husband calling out to her.

One could find many another such story in our parts. After

we stopped butchering the American Indian, we began to sentimentalize him, and the evidence of the Hiawathaization of the Five Nations is to be found in local legends about Lovers' Leaps and Spook Rocks, invariably telling about a pair of yearning lovers and at least one cruel chieftain. These stories have an aura of bookishness, falling somewhere outside the fold of genuine folklore. They are neither the tales the Indians tell of themselves nor tales that have taproots in the white man's past. They are, I suspect, often the product of early local historians and sentimental ladies who were well read and anxious, indeed too anxious, to prove that we in America had had a romantic past. That does not mean that all of the ghostly Indians fall in this rather colorless category; a number of them give evidence of being both more believable as ghosts and more valid as folklore.

Take for example the ghosts of Whoopin' Boys Hollow near Sag Harbor. The eastern end of Long Island is a great crocodile's mouth gnawing at the Atlantic; on the upper jaw is Greenport; where the tongue would rest is Sag Harbor; at the tip of the lower jaw is Montauk Point. In the days before the white man came, a chief lived and died near Greenport whose last command ordered his warriors to carry his body to Montauk for its long rest. Moreover, he insisted that never once should his body touch the ground from the time he left his old home until he reached his last. The braves started out with the litter high upon their shoulders until they came to the section where Sag Harbor is now. By this time they were tired and only the fear inspired by their departed leader prevented their laying down their burden and resting. When they came to a deep and extremely narrow crevice, they saw an opportunity to live up to their dead leader's command and yet take the respite they badly needed. The crevice was narrow enough for them to lay the litter across it in such a way that the body was scores of feet from the earth below. Having followed the letter of their chief's command if not the spirit, they lay down at a little distance to sleep. It wasn't long before a terrifying scream awakened them, the scream of their dead chief as he hurtled off the litter to the rocks far below. What cries of terror and guilty conscience the erstwhile pallbearers let out as they dashed away we do not know, but any youngster in Sag Harbor will tell you that if you pass the spot, you will hear them once again and the old chief crying out to be taken on to Montauk and not left forever halfway to his destination.

A ghost you can hear but not see is never so intriguing as one that puts in a full appearance. Consider the Indian's horse from down in the Southern Tier. The little girl who had this experience has long since been a woman grown, but when she tells of the day she took her father's lunch to him, through the meadows and to the forest's edge, she grows excited and the story flows and rushes. In her girlhood they lived on an isolated farm far from all neighbors. When her father used to work in a field separated from the house by some distance, the child loved to carry his lunch to him. Her father, on the other hand, preferred that some older person accompany her, for the path ran across one meadow and then over a brush fence and into a dense wood. One day she pleaded until her mother packed her off, lunch and all. It was a desolate section then; there were no other houses for miles around, and there were spots like the woods before her

that had never been touched by a white man's axe. The
meadow was clear going. Then she came to the brush fence
over which she must climb to get into the woods. Carefully
she got her footing and began to crawl over the barrier. Just
about halfway over she looked up, and there towering above
her was a mammoth stallion, rearing on his hind legs.

Her father got no lunch that day; he found the neatly
packed basket beside the fence on his way home for dinner.
The little girl had scrambled down a thousand times faster
than she had gone up and run pell-mell for home. Her father
had a satisfactory explanation for the sudden appearance of a
horse in a country where there were none. Their farm was
on land that had once been Indian country, and the red men
were buried all about the place. He believed, and years later
she still believed, that some Indian had buried his horse
nearby and that the spirit of the horse had risen from his
grave that warm summer day to prevent a hidden danger of
the wood from hurting her. It was an explanation which
pleased them and they kept it alive.

In Schenectady they tell of one of the last Mohawks in that
area who died in 1789. His name has not survived, but men
have remembered that in two of the ways of the white man
he excelled his teachers; he could outshoot them and out-
drink them. With these arts mastered he had long moved
among the men of the Dorp with austere familiarity. Now
and then during the year he would bring to town some meat
or fish to exchange for the few articles his simple way of life
required. While he was there he would practice a little drinking and then drift back to his cabin on the Hill of Straw-
berries. On the August day of which I write he made a pres-

ent of his mess of fish to an old friend, refusing anything for it. His explanation was simple and pointed: "Great Spirit call. Indian no need." For once he shunned the tavern and getting into his canoe he started up the Mohawk. Boys who were swimming off a sand bar reported a strange thing later: the canoe moved against the current, driven by no visible power, for the Indian sat in the stern, his head erect, his arms folded serenely across his chest. They were the last to see him alive. No one ever found his body, but the canoe they did find the next day, drifting empty far down the river.

A week later a white man who had known the Indian was

fishing among the river islands when he glanced up and saw
the old Mohawk warrior sitting on the high bank. His arms
were clasped around his knees and his face was turned toward his departed people. The white man thought merely
that the Indian wanted a lift to the mainland and so he rowed
close to the island and invited him to get in the boat. At the
first word, the Mohawk slowly turned his head and faded
from view. Afterward many others saw him, sitting by the
river's edge, always in the same position, his knees hugged to
his chin and his eyes watching the upper reaches of the valley.

Indian massacres of the Revolutionary period have left us
with their ghostly reminders, too. From Cherry Valley and
Cobleskill come tales of the partial re-enactment of those
violences, the screams and shots, the hurrying files of refu-
gees, sad cries in the night. But the story of Nick Wolsey and
his revenge stirs my imagination far more than these frag-
mentary tales. In the early days, close to the Hudson in
Greene County lived a white hunter and fur trader named
Nick Wolsey. He got along well with the Indians in their
nearby village because they could trust him; his dealings with
them were invariably above board and his word was as true
as his aim.

After some little time it may have been observed by the
wise old squaws of the tribe that it was not always beaver
pelts that brought Nick to the encampment. The man whose
sharp eyes could reckon the value of a beaver pelt had looked
carefully at the village lass named Minamee. One day they
were married among her people and then walked down the
valley trail to his snug cabin by the river. Except for the
jealous heart of her forsaken Indian suitor, the marriage was

approved by all her tribesmen. Once there was a sharp, spoken clash between the loser and Wolsey, but it passed and was forgotten as an incident in a day of frolic. The months that followed were full of happy fruitful days for both the bride and groom. Frequently he made trips to the fur traders in Albany and came home with gold in his purse and handsome presents for his wife. By the time a year had swung around there was a small son in the cabin and Nick Wolsey was a happy man.

One evening Nick came back to the cabin after a good day's hunting. Usually the quiet Minamee stood in the doorway, the child in her arms, waiting. No smoke lazed from the chimney and the doorway was empty. It was very silent in the shadow-filled room. Nick stood warily for a moment under the lintel until he saw the baby's head on the floor—bloody, the brown eyes open, the neck a nauseating clot of blood where it had been severed from its body. Deep in the shadow was Minamee, her eyes crazed, her arms clutching the bloody corpse of her child. That night she died, but before that peaceful hour Nick learned of the drunken visit from her unforgetting suitor, who had wreaked his macabre vengeance.

Wolsey had recently been able to purchase a horse, and now he rode to his wife's people. When his account had been heard, the murderer was turned over to him and he bound him tightly with willow withes. Back at the cabin the withes were made still tighter, and then Nick Wolsey conceived a diabolic plan of his own. The Indian had wanted Minamee, but of the woman slim and warm he had made a corpse; well, he could have the corpse. So he bound the living man to the dead woman, tying them both to his horse. He lashed the horse until it became mad with pain and then he loosened it, letting it tear off through the woods, never to be seen again as long as it lived. But sometimes life is not the longest limit and Nick's horse with his grim burden is still galloping down our valley roads. Men see them pass in the dusk and hear the bellowing agony of the Indian, the end of whose punishment is not yet.

Of all the ghost tales of New York, the best known comes to us from the French and Indian Wars and has been told and retold by such masters as Francis Parkman in his *Montcalm and Wolfe* and Robert Louis Stevenson in his *Ticonderoga*. It is the story of a Scottish officer named Duncan Campbell who served under Abercrombie in the campaign of 1758.

Seldom in American history has a general planned more stupidly and acted more cravenly than did General Abercrombie at Ticonderoga, but we must remember that the Scots, English, and Americans who were sacrificed by his fuddleheaded incompetence fought and died with tragic and magnificent courage. With sixteen thousand troops, nine thousand of them Americans, Abercrombie attacked Ticonderoga when it contained fewer than four thousand men, but Montcalm sent him back to Lake George with his tail between his legs, the laughingstock of the provinces. This was the low tide of the war for the enemies of France, but our own attention is turned upon one of the two thousand casualties suffered that day, Major Duncan Campbell of the Black Watch regiment of Scottish Highlanders. He was one of the twenty-six officers in that regiment (out of thirty-seven in all) who left the fields in front of Ticonderoga as a casualty: nine days later he died in the hospital at Fort Edward.

Duncan Campbell was the laird of the castle of Inverawe on the banks of the River Awe, in the Scottish Highlands. In the days after Bonnie Prince Charlie's attempt to take back the British throne for the Stuarts, quarrels and name calling continued in Scotland, sometimes with the sharpest bitterness. One evening a party of gentlemen in the neighborhood of Inverawe became involved in what was at first a political argument and soon turned into a brawl. In the midst of the hot words and drawn swords one man fell to the floor and another sped off in the darkness to rap on the door of Castle Inverawe, asking for sanctuary. True to Scottish traditions of hospitality, the young laird took the fugitive in and hid him in the far recesses of the castle, swearing on his dirk and as head of the clan to protect the man from pursuers.

Almost as soon as he returned to the hall two clansmen brought word to Duncan Campbell that his own cousin Donald had been slain, and he realized that he was protecting his kinsman's murderer. Remembering his oath, he swore he knew nothing of the matter, but the conflict between his loyalty to his oath and his loyalty to his kinsman caused him deep concern. That night his was an uneasy sleep. Sometime in the darkest of the night he opened his eyes to see his cousin Donald standing before him: "Inverawe, Inverawe, Inverawe! blood has been shed. Shield not the murderer." The next morning Campbell made a compromise with his conscience. He spirited his unwelcome guest to a cave on Ben Cruachan, a neighboring height. However well this solution may have satisfied his conscience, it did not please the ghost of his cousin Donald, whose second appearance came that very night, when he repeated his injunction of the night before. We do not know what Duncan Campbell intended to do, but shortly after daylight he went up to the cave, only to find it deserted. That night he slept better than he had on the two preceding, but once more his dead cousin awoke him, less angry this time, but no less decisive in his manner. "Farewell, Inverawe! Farewell, till we meet at Ticonderoga." The word "Ticonderoga" meant nothing to the gentleman, and since his cousin did not reappear, the matter drifted from his mind to be almost forgotten.

He joined the Black Watch soon after this and was busy keeping peace and order in the Highlands. Eventually he became a major and served the regiment well, going with it to America a year or so after the war with France broke out. By this time "Ticonderoga" had come to have a double meaning for him, for while it ever brought back the solemn voice of his ghostly cousin, it had also become in the plans of the army an objective that had to be captured if the French were to be driven from the Colonies. His fellow officers knew the story and did all in their power to prevent him from worrying as they sailed up Lake George with their bright banners flying that July day in 1758. As they camped the night before the battle, his cousin Donald came to him for the last time, saying simply, "Duncan Campbell, we have met at Ticonderoga." He told his fellow soldiers that he would meet his end that day. During one of the gallant, needless charges against the sharply pointed trees the French had cut to form an outer defense of the fort, Duncan Campbell received the wound he died of a few days later.

If 1758 was a bad year for Britain in America, the year 1759 was a far worse year for France; the war that seemed so nearly won at Ticonderoga turned critically against the French. Their defenses formed a triangle with Quebec on the North, Ticonderoga and Crown Point on the east, and Fort Niagara on the west. Frontenac (now Kingston, Ontario), between Quebec and Niagara, fell in 1758, and thus Niagara was left more or less isolated, except as they could call for help from the far western French outposts and their Indian allies. The British sent against them Sir William Johnson. Fort Niagara is situated on a little neck of land which the British cut off from the mainland, then bombarded at will. The two weeks' siege was nerve-racking and terrifying for the French and Indians imprisoned in the fort. Petty jealousies, long-controlled irritations, a thousand annoyances united with the normal fears of battle to make life close to unbearable. It was a bad climate for two French officers who had fallen in love with the same Indian girl, and they finally decided to settle the matter with sabers. In the central courtyard of the fort they faced each other, *en garde*. For a few minutes the besieged Frenchmen and Indians turned their attention from the enemy beyond their walls to the antagonists within. For a moment the sabers made bright arcs of light as they flailed. But it was soon apparent that one swordsman was far better than the other, forcing his opponent back, step by step. Suddenly came a thud as steel cut through flesh and bone and a head bounced along the cobbled pavement, then a splash as the headless body slipped into an open well in the courtyard. Almost before he could lower his dripping saber, the victor faced empty space where but a second before his rival had stood. History does not tell us if this skillful young *sabreur* fell in the action at Niagara, but the shadowy body of his vanquished opponent still can be seen at midnight, rising out of the well and searching the blood-soaked pavement for his long-lost head.

The period of the Revolution fathered a brotherhood of headless ghosts and York State had its full share of them. Long before Irving made the tradition of the galloping Hessian famous, Yorkers were seeing these riders on their roads. They were seen in other parts of the country, too, of course. In the midst of the war two British officers saw one of their own hussars, elegant and soldierly, come riding down Allen's Lane, Philadelphia, carrying his head before him on his saddle. As he reached them, there was a great flash of light and the hussar was nowhere to be seen.

Whether it was the same hussar or another of the clan whom young Hansel met down Warnerville way, I cannot say, but whoever it was things turned out badly for Hansel. Grandma Mary Thurber told the Reverend Wheaton Webb about him when that wise and lovable man was collecting the lore of the Schenevus Valley. It is a story Grandma Thurber had heard from her grandmother, one of the Schoharie Dutch Shafers, about *her* mother's brother and how he came to be a drooling idiot. Hansel was Grandma Thurber's great-grandmother's brother, a stout, good-natured, easygoing, young buck who did the chores, courted the girls, lived a normal farm-filled life. When he heard the old folks tell about spooks and witches as they sat around a winter fire or in the village store, he laughed at them. He had grown up on stories of the Headless Rider who rode a black horse and cast an evil spell over any who got in his way. Every now and then some neighbor claimed that he had seen the Rider, and Hansel's comment was always the same, like a man who has thought up a good answer once and uses it over and over again: "I'd like to meet the Headless Rider some day; I'd trade him my own head for a loaf of bread." Then one day in the woods the headless one came riding down the path and Hansel was far too terrified to offer the exchange he had promised—so terrified, indeed, that when they found him later on, all he could do was look at them with great blue, unknowing, unseeing eyes. Always after that the brain inside his fair head was withered and the spirit dead. A man should measure his adversary before he lays down his challenge.

Not all the ghosts of the Revolutionary period were headless, by any means. In Pine Plains there is a house that was once the Old Drover's Inn, a natural stopping place for cattle drovers going back and forth between the Hudson Valley and Connecticut. For generations there was a noisy ghost in that place who slammed doors and paced up and down, reenacting the movements of his last hours. In life he was a young physician who hung himself the night before he was expected to go into the Continental Army. For many years the rope hung from the rafters, for no one seemed to have the heart to cut it down.

Fort Ontario, near Oswego, goes further: it has an official ghost who dates back to Revolutionary times, for he wears the red coat, white britches, and crossed belts of a British regular. His name is George Fykes and his tombstone can be found in the military cemetery. Tradition has it that Fykes appeared once to every new garrison over a long century, but there have come no reports of troops stationed there during World War II seeing the poor fellow, nor since the State Historian's office has undertaken the preservation of the fort.

Fort Ontario has a second ghost, or did have a few years ago. W. J. Coad, who was stationed at the post in 1919–20 with the Sixty-third Infantry, tells us, "It got so sentries refused to walk Number 2 Post, and a board of officers was convened to make an investigation. After receiving testimony from several sentries, they confessed they had no explanation of the manifestations which had the guard completely disorganized." It began when a guard noticed a light about the size of a saucer following him as he walked his post. At first he thought one of his comrades was playing a trick on him and he ignored the whole matter, saying nothing about it. But the next night another guard served and was concerned to see a light following him. The two men got together and decided that if a trick was being played upon them, then they would do better to say nothing but take matters in their own hands. While one marched the other hid in the recesses of the building and watched. The light came at midnight, just as the City Hall clock struck, and kept pace with the sentry as he walked along. Never ahead nor behind, the light shone brightly over the soldier's head, and as he watched, the second man realized that it would be impossible for any natural light to follow the path that the light was following. Soon the word ran all through the barracks and an increasing number of men objected to guard duty at that time of night; men

who had fought the Germans heroically were taking no
chances with what they were roundly convinced was the spirit
of another soldier who long ago had walked the same post
and now, lonely and restless, had come back to a familiar
duty.

During the Revolution and after, there were a number of
stories about the ghosts that haunted Guy Park and Fort
Johnson, two of the noble houses Sir William Johnson built
along the Mohawk for himself and his son-in-law, Colonel
Guy Johnson. While the Revolution was still in progress
there was a black ghost who appeared in a room in the north-
west part of Fort Johnson, greatly to the annoyance of Colonel Volkert Veeder, whom the Continental authorities had
placed in charge after Guy Johnson and his household departed for Canada and the service of his King. It was at Guy
Park that occurred events which are still puzzling. Soon after
the close of the Revolution the Kennedy family who lived at
Guy Park began seeing at all times of day and night, Polly,
deceased wife of Guy Johnson. What was at first a nuisance
had just about reached the point of alarm when a German
came walking through the valley and inquired if the spirit of
Mrs. Johnson had not been seen there lately. He was told
that indeed she had, that her visits had become so frequent
that one room which the lady seemed to favor had been given
over to her since no one cared to share it with her. More as a
favor to the family than as something he himself wished, the
traveler suggested that he be allowed to spend the night in
the room. When he departed in the morning, seemingly spry
and healthy after his night in the haunted room, he assured
his hosts that the lady would bother them no more; nor did

she. Later the Kennedys began to wonder if they had been bilked, if perhaps they had been the victims of a hoax from beginning to end. There are those who will tell you that this was a carefully worked-out scheme, based on the credulity of the Kennedy family, to recover the treasure which the Johnsons hid in the house before they left. According to this theory, the ghost was really the living servant of Mrs. Johnson, wearing her dead mistress's clothes, delegated to scare the family out of the room where the valuables were secreted. The spook-laying German was either a part of the plan, or an interloper who knew what was afoot and beat the rightful owners to the snatch. Of course, those who take their ghosts straight will have none of this theorizing, and will merely believe that the German, versed in Old World *Hexerei*, was able to rid the house of its supernatural tenant and out of the greatness of his heart did so.

Half a century later Fort Johnson was haunted by quite a different spirit. Early in the last century a store stood near the fort, where one night a drunken fellow got in a fight with the storekeeper, assaulting him and hurting him severely. But the storekeeper was still full of fight; he grabbed a gun and chased his assailant out of the store, up the street to the fort. There the man ducked into the big house, running, terrified now, up the stairs to the attic. As the drunk reached the attic door, the grocer aimed and fired. The body came tumbling down to his feet; on the walls were tiny rivulets of blood that had spattered when the man was struck. The corpse was taken to the cellar and placed (this is the only unbelievable part of the tale) in a cask of whisky, where it stayed until spring. As the ice began to break, the barrel was rolled to the

river's edge and then sent on its way to the sea. The dead man's ghost claimed a room in the fort for many years, and according to the testimony of the Wilson family, who thought for a while of renting the place, it became noisy and bothersome, banging doors and, in the cellar, opening one door as soon as another closed. A daughter of the Wilsons claimed later to have owned a photograph of the Fort Johnson ghost. She said it was all in white, standing by a door. When I last heard the photograph had been misplaced, but it ought to turn up any day now.

Another story that has come to us from the Revolutionary

period is the oft-repeated account of the Horseman of Leeds. Every Greene County historian has had his own version, and seemingly, every citizen of the country around Leeds has his version. There is no separating chaff from wheat in this matter; rather, you choose what grains you like and grind out your own flour. What follows is a composite containing the essential features of many of the tellings and a selection of details that suit my personal taste, for this is the manner in which men tell this tale.

The village of Leeds lies in the foothills of the Catskills, up from the Hudson River Valley a few miles. It was settled early, and by the time of the Revolution it had living in or near it a number of prosperous citizens, among whom the Salisbury family were perhaps the most prosperous. Surrounded by a thousand upland acres, they lived in a large stone house which had been built in 1705. Throughout much of the eighteenth century the owner of this property was an arbitrary, overbearing man named William Salisbury, who ruled his slaves and indentured servants with a will that insisted on obedience, unquestioning and immediate. Among the latter group was a young German girl named Anna Swartz, who was paying with service for her passage from the old country. She was a gay, laughter-loving girl who enjoyed merry parties and the new ways of dancing she found here, which were even better than the old village dances at home. There was little or no gaiety on the Salisbury farm, and about her only satisfactions came from the milch cows which she enjoyed bringing in from pasture with a little dog that had adopted her soon after her arrival at the farm. The hours she labored were long and tedious, and the relaxations were rare indeed. Not far from the center of Leeds, there lived a good-natured, good-for-nothing German family whose door was always ajar to whatever lighthearted person wanted to come in. It was not a place calculated to encourage sobriety, virtue, or industry, but the people who went there had a lot of fun. Salisbury learned that when she could sneak away, Anna was going there, and he made it vividly clear that she should go no more.

One night soon after this, word came up to him that the girl had sneaked off the farm and headed for Leeds. This was the last of a series of petty irritations; there was a streak of insubordination in the girl that needed disciplining. Such a spirit and such actions could lead to trouble, and William Salisbury had had enough. He strode to the barns and ordered a horse saddled while he went into the harness room to pick up a ten- or twelve-foot rope. He jumped on the horse and streaked to the village. He pulled up short at the house of laughter and dismounted. For a moment he stood in the doorway, liking what he saw even less than he had expected. He called Anna by name and she came to him, half in fear, half in anger.

The group in the house came to the door, and in the light which flooded past them into the dooryard, they saw this man, whose every motion betrayed his anger, tying one end of his rope around Anna's waist, the other to the girth of his saddle. He worked silently, speaking neither to the girl nor her companions. He did not even glance up as he slipped his foot into the stirrup and swung up into the saddle. He would humiliate this girl, and teach her and her hoyden friends that he meant to be obeyed.

The horse was still walking as they left the yard, but Salisbury touched its flank lightly with his heel until it had struck up a leisurely jog trot. Soon the girl was panting, running as fast as her weary legs would carry her. Then, in the darkness she stumbled on a rock in the road; as she fell, the sudden tugging on the girth frightened the horse. First a leap, and then his hooves were pounding down the country road. Anna screamed, and her body was hurled bumping and bouncing at the end of the rope. Salisbury tried to stop the horse, but in one of its wild leaps he was thrown into the ditch. He sat up, bruised and shaken, to see two spots of light, bobbing and weaving in the darkness, the white rump of the horse and the body of the girl.

Salisbury was by nature and instinct on the side of the law, and he reported the accident to the proper authorities. He was tried and convicted of murder and ordered to be hung, but the sentence was not to be carried out until he was ninety-nine years old. Until that time he was to wear a halter about his neck as a perpetual reminder of his ordered fate. A lenient judge permitted the rope to become a silken cord in time, but his was a lonely life, isolated from his friends and neighbors. The people began to avoid the road by his farm after dark if they could, because too many had seen the white horse and the bounding white form racing through too many nights to be comfortable. Long after they all had died, her favorite milch cow mooed and the little dog moaned as the horse and girl passed by. Strangest of all was the womanly figure that appeared on a rock near where Anna died. It would sit and sing wildly, cry out and laugh hysterically as it gazed at the lighted candle on each finger. Salisbury grew to be an old man before his time, but he lived on, reporting to the courthouse each year, just as he had been ordered to do. The year he was ninety-nine he went as usual, but the judge who tried him, all the jurors and the witnesses, everybody was long since in his grave. There was no one in the year 1800 who felt called upon to carry out the sentence, so the old man went back to his farm, the long years fulfilled, and yet death did not come. When he had lived a full century he died, and after that, when the horse ran in the moonlight there was a rider astride, and so it has been for a century and a half.

Of all the different ways to exorcise a ghost, flames are the most effective. This was how the Mansion House at Sodus Point on Lake Ontario finally was rid of Asher Warner. When the British troops came swooping down upon that snug harbor town on a June day in 1813, they found a people who had grown weary waiting for their foe. The attack had long been expected, so long that the militia sent to defend the best harbor on Lake Ontario had gone off about other business, and the townsmen had settled back to chuckle over the attack that had never materialized. Then they came, ninety ships with their cannon and their cargoes of troops. Townspeople and the handful of militia who could be collected fought well, but they fought a pitifully hopeless battle. When the ships set sail again, they left utter desolation, for their task had not been to take and hold a beachhead, but to make useless to their enemy a point of departure for expeditions against themselves. Only one house still stood; all the others were smoldering ruins. That one remained because a British officer had not had the heart to disturb a young American soldier, Asher Warner, who was dying of his wounds and lay in that house. They gave him a pitcher of water and left him. The bloody prints of his hands upon the walls were seen by men yet living who could well imagine his pathetic attempts to rise to his feet and join the battle once again. And they saw on the floor bloodstains that never came off. Asher Warner stayed in the house where he died long years after they buried him in his grave, long after Sodus Point was rebuilt and the foe became our friend. Only the flames which destroyed the aged house could put him to final rest.

One of the most fertile areas for ghost lore in New York State is the section within a mile radius of Lindenwald, the home of Martin Van Buren, on the outskirts of Kinderhook. We should remember that it was while staying at Lindenwald that Irving heard the legend of the Headless Horseman, which he moved to Sleepy Hollow when he came to write it. If he had told the story as taking place in its Columbia County locale, we would not be surprised to find the area so ghost-ridden, but he took his yarn and his locale and gave it a life of its own in the part of the valley he loved so well. The Van Alen house built in 1737 a mile east of Kinderhook is described to the last timber as the home of the Van Tassels. For many years the place has been boarded up, and I recall a pleasant summer's afternoon when Harold Thompson, the dean of New York's folklorists, and I prowled around the place, peeking into windows and attempting, ineffectually, a minor case of illegal entry. We were prepared to wait until midnight when a rider whom neighbor folk believe to be Merwin, the original for Ichabod Crane, could be expected to gallop off the concrete of Route 9H and turn down the driveway leading to the house. We were prepared for him to ride as far as the leaning pine, growing where a trickling stream flows under a driveway, and then we expected him to disappear. Midnight was only six hours away, and it seemed to me that the wait would be well worth while, but alas for the ambitions of scholars! The two ladies who accompanied us made it clear they would have none of it; they were hungry, even if we didn't realize that we were, too. We knew when we were defeated.

Less than a mile to the south along 9H, behind great masses of undergrowth hides Lindenwald, an architectural hodgepodge standing as monument to the taste of the mid-nineteenth century. The home that Judge William Peter Van Ness built in 1797 was a solid, well-balanced brick house of the postcolonial period. Its central hall and generous stairway gave the impression of gentility and hospitality that the owner no doubt hoped to achieve. When Martin Van Buren retired from the presidency, he bought the place from the family of Judge Van Ness, under whom he had studied law. Nine years later, Richard Upjohn, who had just completed Trinity Church in New York, remodeled and enlarged the house. He added a steep front gable, a rococo porch, a scalloped cornice, Italianate bell tower, and wings on the south and west. Today the visitor is impressed by the imported wallpaper of Van Buren's period, the Brussels carpets retaining their warm reds and yellows. The last time I visited Lindenwald many of the former President's possessions were still there. Sometime the State will take over the place, as it should, but when that day comes a quality will inevitably be lost. The unmowed lawns, the weed-filled driveway, the great, brooding trees that tower over the yard and outhouses give the place an eerie and romantic quality. Friends of mine who have lived there tell of shutters that unexpectedly bang in the night, footsteps that slowly climb the stairs, weird noises that drift through the house, aided, perhaps, by the hot-air heating system that was installed in 1834 and seven fireplaces all connecting with one chimney.

Two of the ghosts that haunt Lindenwald were famous men in their times, one a Vice-president, the other a President, of this country, for the people tell of having seen or tell of others having seen both Aaron Burr and Martin Van Buren in and about the premises. Aaron Burr, it will be remembered, was a friend of the Van Buren family, and William Van Ness was his second in the ill-fated duel with Hamilton. There is one tradition that Burr came to Lindenwald after the duel, but the evidence does not support this. That he was a visitor there in the Van Ness times, however, is not at all unlikely. When he appears, and both servants of the house and neighboring farmers are said to have seen him, he wears the lace cuffs and wine-colored coat, the suave smile that nearly won him an empire. One who saw him told of the wind blowing a ripping gale as Burr walked through the orchard at Lindenwald, but it seemed not to touch him, and there was no movement of the long lace cuffs, as if there were an island of stillness about the little man.

The orchard is almost as ghost-ridden as the house, for both Martin Van Buren and his butler, as well as Burr, have been reported at different times under the apple trees. The butler was a hardened toper who used to sneak off to the apple trees to have a quiet snifter until one day, after an argument, he went out to the orchard, not for refreshment, but to hang himself. Then there was a woman who was murdered near the gatehouse, and within the last generation her lonely, white figure, too, has been seen moving about in the shadows.

There were a goodly number of Negroes in the Kinderhook area, several of whom worked at Lindenwald. Aunt Sarah was a vigorous, strong-minded martinet who ruled the Van Buren kitchen with an iron hand and a genius for fine cooking. She ruled it in solitary glory much of the time, permitting other servants to enter only when they had her permission, and then they were expected to leave as soon as possible. Residents have told me that early on Sunday mornings there still drifts up from the empty kitchen one of the most delectable smells to be enjoyed in America, the lovely fragrance of pancakes cooking on a buttered griddle—this at times when the fires are dead in the stove and the kitchen empty of all living persons. I cannot help but wonder if maybe the old cook doesn't come back and stir a weird batter to drop upon a departed griddle over a fire that went out long ago. But the pancakes have nothing to do with Tom who was the servant of a Mrs. Wagner and a neighbor of Lindenwald. Aunt Sarah, in her time, died, then Martin Van Buren died, and the family left the vacant house in charge of Mrs. Wagner until a buyer could be found. At last word came that the new owners were soon to appear, and it seemed advisable to put the house in order. Mrs. Wagner told Tom to go over to the big house and get the kitchen in shape, but Tom had known Aunt Sarah all too well, and he was not sure it was wise to intrude upon one who had been so explicit about her rights and her domain. After a deal of muttering Tom went, but his stay was short. He reported: "I went down into the cellar and then into the kitchen, but the minute I took up a pan I heard a sound. As I looked up, down the chimney came Aunt Sarah. She was covered with soot, but her eyes were blazing, and the ends of her kerchief stood up on her head just like horns. So I said to myself, 'Tom, you're getting out of this cellar as fast as you can, and nobody's going to make you go back.'" Tom never did go back, and if the pancakes are hers, there must still be times when she rules her kitchen.

Another story takes us a mile or so west of Lindenwald to the old brick school built on a little triangle of land formed by Route 9 and another road from near the Van Buren estate. Aunt Sally, a character known to many a present-day adult in the Kinderhook section when they were children, had two sons, unbelievably nicknamed Woodchuck Pete and Cottage Joe. The old lady shared a belief with many Americans that if you want to find buried treasure, you should do your digging at a crossroads, that you should, meanwhile, observe absolute silence. She got a notion that there was buried treasure near the old schoolhouse, and matriarch that she was, she ordered the boys to collect picks, shovels, crowbars, and come with her on the night she felt the moon was just right. When they reached the spot where she was positive they would find their fortune, she told them to start digging, to keep on digging no matter what happened, and not to say a word. They were used to doing what she told them, and soon the dirt was flying. Pretty soon Cottage Joe's pick hit something that gave out a hollow sound: just at that very moment, as they straightened up to ease their backs, they saw old Uncle Pete come walking down the side road. Uncle Pete had been dead for years, but the boys went right on with their digging; if the old man wanted to watch them that was no affair of theirs. Now they began to shovel the dirt off the top of a chest, a very old oaken piece with iron bands around it. As they dug the dirt away from the corner of the box, they were attracted by the sight of a newcomer approaching, a man riding a huge black horse, carrying his head in his lap. The horse breathed out billows of smoke from his nostrils, and when he walked sparks flew from his hooves. The man rode around and around them, but nobody said a word, and both boys kept on digging. As they neatly cleared the dirt from the sides of the chest they realized that dozens of Aunt Sally's dead friends and kinfolk stood by Uncle Pete, watching, waiting. In the moonlight they drove the crowbars down on either side of the box and put all their strength to the task. Their mother stood watching them, feeling every move they made, silently, prayerfully urging them on. Now the chest moved in its hole. While one of them held it, the other slipped a rope underneath; twice around it went, and they wordlessly tugged at either side. One end rose, and Joe stepped forward to get a better grip, but as he did, the rope slipped in his sweating hand and the gold-filled chest hit his foot with a terrific weight. A heartfelt "Damn!" came impulsively from his lips, and as he spoke, the haunted gold slid back into its hole, the dirt rolled down after it,the sod they had so carefully piled to the side eased itself into place. Just at that instant a small cloud drifted past the moon, and when the light cleared again, Uncle Pete, the horseman, the old departed friends were no longer there. There was nothing to do but go home; never again could they hope to dig for treasure in that place. So two weary boys and a heartsick mother went slowly down the home road, listlessly dragging the tools that were to have made them rich beyond all dreams.

A distinguished North Country contemporary of Martin Van Buren has put in an appearance in recent times in a unique and very imaginative manner. I like a ghost that has a fresh approach to his problem and eschews the hackneyed rappings and tappings by which dull fellows make their presence known; Dr. Samuel Guthrie of Sackets Harbor is a ghost to my taste. It was Dr. Guthrie who in 1831 made important discoveries relative to the manufacture of chloroform. He manufactured "S. Guthrie's Waterproof Priming." He invented the punchlock musket, and a method for converting potato starch into sugar. His was obviously a rich and curious mind that was not satisfied with the well-worn and routine ways of doing things.

It began ten years ago when the family that lived in the house the doctor had built in Sackets Harbor heard bones rattle in the closet where he had kept his skeletons. But that, as they realized later, was merely a curtain raiser for what was coming. On the evening when the grandfather of the family lay dying, his wife stayed silently with him, easing the hard passage. She stood at the foot of the bed, slightly leaning on the footboard, her hands folded before her. She could not have told you how long her gaze had been searching the pallid face of her husband when she sensed that they were no longer alone. She looked to the side of the bed, and there stood a white-haired man attired in clothes long out of date. She recognized him immediately as Dr. Guthrie, for she had been familiar with pictures of the builder of their home. The suddenness of his coming, and under such circumstances, was too much for the overwrought woman: she screamed and then fainted. When members of the family rushed into the room, they discovered her lying on the floor, but what was even more curious was that the whole place was permeated by the odor of chloroform, although there was not an ounce of the drug in the house, nor had there been throughout the old gentleman's illness. When they had picked up his wife and begun to revive her, they turned their attention to him. He was dead.

There must have been a time when one could have garnered a rich harvest of ghostly tales along that romantic thread of water, the Erie Canal. Not many have come down to me, none very interesting. In the Rome Swamp one night a young mule driver saw an awful white form rise out of the towpath; it had a horrible face and great flashing teeth. The boy struck out at it over and over again with a stick he carried, but it landed on nothing solid. This kind of incident was told by old-timers, sitting around an evening fire by a string of tied-up boats. Another might corroborate such an incident with his own memories of a similar fearsome critter he had seen while spending the night in one of the many canal-side taverns. Someone else in the group would have heard of a canal captain who cut the throat of his cook and

threw her body into the water. He would give them well-documented reports of local farm folk who still could hear her last scream on the anniversary of the deed. Another would tell of a ghost to be seen along railroad tracks down where a spur of the Shenandoah and Susquehanna Railroad runs to one of the Pennsylvania lumber camps. When the spur was being built, two of the workers got into a fight and one of them was killed. Afterward, on moonlight nights men saw the winner tote the dead man along the tracks in a wheelbarrow, his feet hanging over one side and his head over the other. The connoisseur of ghosts will be pleased to note here the rather unusual circumstance of a ghostly corpse, for this is a re-enactment of the moments after the man had been killed, and so there is seen, or if you wish to be technical, there is said to be seen, the ghostly spirit of a corpse. I know of one other somewhat similar case. Down in Middletown the corpse of a suicide has been seen a good many times hanging from the tree where he died.

Slavery, the Underground Railroad, and the Civil War provide the backgrounds for a number of stories which are still current in my state. While there was no slavery in New York after 1827, there are records of slaves being sold as late as 1814 in the village of Altamont. The story of the Simmons slaves comes from but a few miles farther up in the Helderbergs in the village of Berne. The central figure is a man named Simmons, a Southerner from his speech and ways; indeed, he made a point of his ancient lineage, and he passed for what he called himself, a Southern aristocrat. Why such a one as he purported to be should leave the warmth of his homeland for the mocking blizzards of Berne seemed not at all unusual to the natives; rather, it confirmed their first favorable impression of the fellow, showed him to possess sound judgment. He brought with him a dozen or more slaves to work the six-hundred-acre farm he secured. The brick building where he quartered them still stands, almost as solid as it was in the years just before the War of 1812, when Simmons built it. He was an enterprising man and fitted in well with the community, where the trend was toward industrialization. Not to be outdone by his neighbors, he began building an axe factory, the earliest in that part of

Albany County. With his suave courtliness he soon persuaded the fattest pockets in town to invest in the venture, but it wasn't long before the factory stood empty, the venture a failure, and Simmons and his household moved off to greener clover. How many of his household went with him was a moot point. People said there weren't half as many slaves when he left as when he arrived, and others, that he had mistreated the Negroes badly, throwing them down a deep, dry well to punish them and some of them died there. Then, on rainy nights, men saw black-faced ghosts walking slowly around the well, heads down, eyes averted. A later owner had the well filled in with rocks but, for a century after, children were advised to stay away from that part of the yard, especially when it was raining.

From a later period and a more southerly part of our state comes word of a station on the Underground Railroad where tragedy has left us another ghostly heritage. There is a house down in Emmons, not far from the Susquehanna, which served, as did so many York State homes, as a way station for courageous colored men and women who were willing to gamble their lives for freedom. A tunnel led from the house to the river, but it was hastily dug, and in some parts the clay walls were only held in place by wooden props. One spring after the rains had saturated the earth, the walls were weakened and on a certain night the tunnel came crumbling down, trapping forever five or six Negroes who had just arrived. Their screams and cries could be heard at both ends of the tunnel, and even, faintly, above ground. On spring nights when the frost is out of the ground and the rains have begun to fall, they are still heard occasionally, these voices of casualties in the long battle for human liberty.

In every war there are always some soldiers who do not come home with their comrades, but who, in their own good time, return from the far-off soil where they lie buried. New York sent half a million men to the armies of Abe Lincoln and it is only reasonable to expect that a few of them should be among the restless dead. In Salem, in Washington County, they tell of the Good Gray Ghost, a soldier in the War of the Rebellion, who was for many years a familiar spirit in the town. No one feared him; no one had reason to. A Miss Kathryn Tierney of Albany used to work in his home when she was a girl, and she remembers a summer evening when she was walking alone in the garden and the Gray Ghost approached her and called her by name. Like the others, she wasn't scared, for it all seemed too natural, and he was far too courteous and gentle in his demeanor to frighten anyone. It must have been that he missed the gaiety he had known in his youth, because there was hardly ever a party or big dinner in the house but some one guest would see him standing in the shadows wistfully watching the fun. Time brings changes even for those of the spirit world, and some years ago the house was torn down to make room for a new school and, as often happens, when his haunt was demolished, the ghost no longer returned. There is a minor controversy among the small fry of Salem as to whether a careful midnight watch within the school would bring them face to face with the figure their fathers and grandfathers knew. My advice is against the experiment; it is most unusual for a ghost to change his habitation. On the other hand, no one can afford these days to stand in the way of true scientific inquiry.

A New York couple who moved to Jersey had a curious experience with the ghost of a man who had starved to death in their house during the Civil War. Whether he was a spy or an escaped Confederate prisoner is uncertain, but that he starved to death was certain. The real-estate man warned them about him when they first took the house, but they were young and very much in love; it didn't seem likely that they would be bothered. Nor were they, once they got adjusted to George. In a way, he became a silent member of the family, never in the way, but always about the premises. They could hear him at night, prowling about the kitchen, getting himself a snack, plodding back and forth between the stove and the kitchen table. As dusk fell during the winter, the young wife getting supper in the kitchen would hear the front door open and footsteps go down the cellar stairs; then the furnace door would open. She would call out, "Is that you, dear?" knowing full well that it would be another half-hour before her husband would enter the front door, go down the cellar stairs to fix the furnace. She felt better about it if she made sure each time, and her question never perturbed George, nor did he ever answer. It was their guests who saw George. They would awaken in the night, and there they would see him across the guest bedroom, bent nearly double as if in wretched pain, pacing back and forth, over and over again. Some of their guests stayed only one night, but others grew as used to him as their hosts. Not a bad fellow once you caught on to his ways.

There was a legend current in Albany during my youth which Mary Raymond Shipman Andrews made into a very successful short story called "The White Satin Dress." It will be remembered that in Lincoln's party on the evening he was shot there was a young couple whose engagement had recently been announced: Major Henry Reed Rathbone, whose family were partners in the successful firm of stove makers, Rathbone, Sard and Company, and Miss Clara Harris, the daughter of one of Albany's most distinguished citizens, United States Senator Ira Harris. It was certainly the most terrible night of Miss Harris's life, and for years afterward its every moment stood clear in her memory. There was the play, the shot that echoed through the theatre, the splashing of blood, Major Rathbone's valiant attempt to catch the murderer, the flash of Booth's knife as it stabbed her fiancé, the leap onto the stage, her own presence of mind as she called out for water for the President. Time softened the pangs of the tragedy, and sometimes it was but as a nightmare dimly remembered. This was especially true after she returned to Albany and became Major Rathbone's bride. There was one memento, however, that could bring the whole evening back to her on bitter wings; that was the satin dress she had had made for the occasion. Never again could she bring herself to wear it, nor to dispose of it. It hung by itself in her closet, spotted with the blood of the nation's beloved President and of her own beloved husband. Eventually the Rathbones decided to move from the home where the dress had long hung. There was considerable discussion about it: should Clara destroy it, or take it with her? For reasons of her own she did not want to see it moved from its place. A solution was hit upon; the lady moved out of her old home satisfied that she had made the best possible disposal of the gown. This much of the story I knew as a boy.

Mrs. Andrews's story deals with descendants of the family which next occupied the house. They were related to a Governor of Massachusetts, who, on one occasion, came to visit. The Governor was faced with a difficult decision: a bill had been passed by his legislature which he believed important for his state's welfare, but it had provoked a major political storm. It seemed unlikely that he could be re-elected if he signed it and he could rationalize a veto easily enough. It was the old question of whether to act like a politician or a statesman. A man whose ambitions struggle with his conscience doesn't sleep well, and the executive lay long in the guest bedroom trying to resolve his conflict. At length he slept, only to awaken with a start. There was someone in the room with him; he raised himself on his elbow to see standing in the moonlight the figure of Lincoln, calm, patient, and with an understanding smile upon his lips. Then the presence was gone, and the Governor was alone with the moonlight. He was wide awake now and he moved to turn on the light, during which he knocked over on the floor a volume of Lincoln's speeches which had been on the stand by his bed. As he picked it up he saw the words, "Hew honestly to the line; let the Lord take care of the chips." Then he knew that he would sign the controversial bill, and he did sign it. To his surprise he was re-elected that fall to serve his state even more ably than he had before. His hosts, in the meantime, had learned his story only to be puzzled by it, or to put it down to the delusions of a tired and overwrought mind. Later they were not so sure, for when they came to do some remodeling in that part of the house, they found a tiny closet completely sealed off from the room where their guest had spent his troubled night and in the closet was the gown with the stains of Lincoln's blood upon it.

When I first heard of the ghost train which runs one day each April up the Harlem Division of the New York Central Railroad, it sounded to me suspiciously like the famous train that carried Lincoln's body on the long voyage home in the April of '65. When I told Carl Sandburg about it, he suggested that I look in Lloyd Lewis's *Myths After Lincoln,* where indeed, I discovered that Mr. Lewis had published the story. His version was remarkably like mine and had been found in an Albany newspaper of a generation ago, where it was reported as part of the folklore of our area. The principal difference between his account and mine was that in his the train was reported running on the Hudson River Division of the New York Central where it belonged.

There are two trains, actually; the engines of both are old-timers with wide smokestacks and much polished brass. Their entire lengths are draped with crêpe, giving the impression of great shrouds on wheels. In the first train there is neither engineer nor fireman in the cab, but on one of the several flatcars which follow the engine there is a large band soundlessly playing its instruments; over the years the players have lost all flesh and now are only skeletons. The first train is followed by a second, this time with a single flatcar, draped as is the one before it, but on this car is a lonely coffin, nothing more, neither ghost nor skeleton. As the first train approaches, a black carpet seems to unroll along the track before it and all sound is blanketed. Men know which day in spring the ghost trains have passed through, for all clocks stop and wait five to eight minutes before they begin again. It must be that the eyes of men are no longer as keen as they used to be, for there are only a few of the old-timers left who know why one day each April the trains are all late as they pull into Chatham. There can be no doubt that it is Lincoln's train, divided into two sections, but what ghostly dunderhead has switched it up the Harlem Division, instead of up the Hudson River Division where it belongs?

War also breeds stories in which the returning dead seem so like the living that they are mistaken for them, and World War II was no exception. The reasons are simple enough to fathom: it is then that families are separated, that death strikes indiscriminately among the men who have gone to the services; civilians and servicemen alike think in terms of death each hour of every day.

For example, there is a story they told in Auburn about a young man of that city named Captain "Brick" Barton. Captain Barton was the pilot of one of the B-24's operating from English bases in the spring of 1943. He was very popular with his crew, and despite the fact that they had suffered a number of losses from flak and enemy pursuit planes, their morale was high. Their most recent loss was Barton's copilot, who had been hospitalized after the last raid, so that it was a very young lieutenant on his first combat mission who sat beside Brick as they took off for Frankfurt. They found their target, dropped their load, and had just turned for home when machine-gun fire from a German pursuit plane ripped through the plastic glass, spattering Brick's blood over the instrument panel and everything else in sight. Another burst ripped into the controls, so that the young copilot took over and began to fly home a badly messed-up bomber. The captain was entirely conscious and his mind was remarkably alert for a man who had taken the punishment he had. Sitting in his seat, completely relaxed, he refused to go back where there was more room and where he could lie down. His mind was on the plane, and as the weather grew soupier and the motors responded with less and less enthusiasm to the copilot's touch, Brick kept giving him helpful suggestions, fruits of twenty missions over the Reich. For fifty-seven minutes the wise veteran and the youthful novice kept the plane coming straight through to the field from which they had departed. As they neared their radio tower, the copilot signaled for an ambulance, for the sudden silence beside him reminded him of the beating Brick had taken when the bullets came streaming through the plane. No sooner had they come to a stop and the copilot climbed down, than the flight surgeon appeared. He complimented the lieutenant on the way he had brought the damaged ship in. "I never could have done it, sir, if Captain Barton hadn't given me pointers all the way back from Frankfurt." The crew gathered beside the big plane, but only for a second, for the physician who had gone up to look Brick over was on the ground almost immediately. He looked at the men, and then for a long second at the lieutenant, before he spoke: "Men, I am afraid I can be of no help to Captain Barton. He was killed instantly and has been dead now for nearly an hour."

One evening during the war we were having dinner with John Jacob Niles, the ballad singer. He had just returned from a cross-country tour and we were swapping ghost tales.

He would tell one and I would tell one; we were having a wonderful time. During a pause in the conversation when I was bludgeoning my brains to match a beautifully told story of his to which we had all listened with horrified delight, the quiet voice of another guest, Mrs. Richard Eldredge, broke the silence. "I heard a strange story in New York last week." She paused, as though she were unwilling to trust herself with the facts. But this is the story she told.

A gentleman named Oswald Remsen was in New York on business. As usual, he stayed at the Harvard Club and regularly ate his dinners there. He was on his way thither for what he feared would be a solitary meal when a red light prevented his crossing Broadway at Forty-fourth Street. As he waited he noticed two officers of the R.A.F. right beside him; they seemed to be checking their wrist watches against the time flashed on the New York Times Building.

One of them turned to him and asked, "Excuse me, sir, but is this Times Square?"

He assured them that it was and the three of them walked across town together. The officers were full of questions, once they got over a basic shyness. It was, he discovered, their first trip to New York and they found it very exciting after the restrictions of England. He remembered afterward that every block or so one or the other of them would look at his wrist watch, although this didn't impress him very much at the time. A few blocks east he asked if they had any plans for dinner. No, they were quite free. Wouldn't they like to dine with him at his club? That was very nice of him and they would be delighted. But as they spoke one of them took a covert look at his watch; they looked at each other and nodded.

It was a good dinner, with coffee and brandy and cigars over which to linger. They talked of the war, of England, of Oxford where Mr. Remsen had spent a pleasant, youthful year. They even discovered a casual acquaintance in common. They were, he discovered, in the bomber command, but like many in similar situations, they had no inclination to talk about that. And every little while one or the other of them would take a quick look at his watch. Once Mr. Remsen asked rather timidly if he were keeping them from an appointment elsewhere. They assured him they were having a fine time. They talked about England and America, what made them different and in what ways they were alike. They talked of the world after the war, and their hopes for it. It was the mature conversation of three intelligent men, different in backgrounds, in ages and in outlooks, but united in their good will and values.

At five minutes before midnight they looked at their watches simultaneously and both of them arose.

"Sir, we thank you very much; you have been very kind to us. In one way it has been the strangest evening of our lives, you know."

"I don't think I understand," said Mr. Remsen slowly.

"No, of course not. But you see, sir, just twenty-four hours ago Bill, here, and I were killed over Berlin. And now we have to be getting back. Good night and thank you."

And with that, both of them disappeared.

There is an American folk classic told during the Spanish American War and World War I, which both Alexander

Woollcott and Bennett Cerf have reported, but it was told during World War II in a version more timely and, to my taste, more touching. I heard it on a day coach of the New York Central from a woman who happened to sit next to me from Syracuse to Lyons. She assured me that the circumstances were perfectly true. The woman in the story had been known to friends of hers in the naval base where her own husband had but recently been stationed, and whence she was returning home.

Lieutenant Crockfield entered the Navy from civilian life a few months before Pearl Harbor, and so he saw a good many of those early, disheartening battles of the Pacific war. His ship was damaged in one of these conflicts and put into a Pacific Coast repair base where it stayed for several months. While these repairs were going on, Mrs. Crockfield joined her husband for the best weeks of their lives. He went back to sea, and she took a small apartment by herself to await the birth of their child. Letters came quite regularly, considering that her husband was assigned to a force that was unusually active. She kept her mind away from the possibility that anything could really happen to her husband; tragedy might strike the husbands of her friends, yes, but never her husband. The daughter who was born to her was a delight, and her letters detailed every new development. His in reply asked a thousand questions and spoke repeatedly of his yearning to see his wife and the daughter who had come to them.

One evening as she sat by herself rereading the letter that had arrived that morning, she heard a noise in the child's room. She went over and opened the door. There in the half-light stood her husband in his tropical uniform, looking down at the child. As she started to cry out his name, he walked swiftly to the door at the opposite end of the room and, without opening it, passed through to the other side. After her first excitement and sinking alarm, she came back to stand by the infant's bed. At her feet she noticed a pool of water, and as she knelt to examine it she observed something green floating in it. She picked it up and put it between two blotters. Later, after the inevitable telegram from the Navy Department had come, she took the blotters and the green thing to a friend of her father's who taught marine botany in one of the California universities. He recognized it after some careful checking in the library. It was a fairly uncommon type of seaweed, found in the South Pacific, where it grows only on the bodies of the dead.

CHAPTER SIX

The Ghostly Hitchhiker

In general we tend to think of folklore as only the oral
tradition current among unsophisticated people. What we
frequently forget is that there is also an oral tradition among
all sorts and classes of people. The commonest examples from
sophisticated circles are off-color stories, but there is also an
oral tradition of tales of the supernatural which often crop
up during the talk after a good dinner. We might call these
"urban ghost tales." The three stories from World War II
in the previous chapter are good examples.

Stories of this sort not infrequently find their way into print and there may well be an interplay between the oral stream and the printed page. The late Alexander Woollcott, Carl Carmer, and Bennett Cerf have published stories which they heard among their friends—indeed, they have published variants of the same stories—but try to find some teller who first met his favorite yarn in print. Always a cousin from Long Island heard it from his landlady who knew one of the participants.

We might note some of the characteristics. These stories are usually told by persons of some education; the timing and order of events betray an awareness of literary form. The stories are told by people who do not, generally speaking, accept the supernatural. The manner of telling is matter-of-fact, but filled with details which give the impression of reality and truth. The implication of the style is: "You may not believe this story. I hardly did myself when I first heard it, but this is what happened." The supernatural elements are played down rather than emphasized. The voice does not change its pitch for the climax but remains quietly confidential and prosaically matter-of-fact. It isn't until the shock of the climax has passed that the mind rejects what it has heard.

The classic example of urban ghost lore is generally called "The Ghostly Hitchhiker" or sometimes "Hitchhiking Hattie." It has been growing and thriving in America for nearly seventy years but came to full flower thirty-odd years ago. Its widespread distribution, its acceptance, its curious, piquant appeal, give it a special place in American folklore.

I recall the first time I heard of the ghostly hitchhiker. It

must have been about 1920 when my father came home for
lunch one noon and told us of a book salesman who had been
in that morning with a story about a strange experience a
friend of his brother had recently had.

The man had been to a party out in the country near
Albany. About midnight he had bid his host and hostess good
night and started for home in a torrential autumn downpour.
He was driving a coupe, the right door of which was jammed
in such a way that it was impossible to open it. He went
slowly down the highway, peering intently through the area
the windshield wiper made clean for him. As he started to
pass Graceland Cemetery he noticed a girl standing by the
big gates; she was young and slightly built, and she wore a
thin white evening dress. Although she did not signal him
in any way, he had the feeling that only her innate dignity
prevented her from doing so. He pulled up the car and, after
rolling down the window, asked her if she would care to ride
into town. In a quiet voice she thanked him and admitted
that she would appreciate a lift. Because the right-hand door
was broken, he got out of the car and let the girl slide under
the wheel to her seat.

The rain was coming down now in torrents, and the man
was so engrossed with his driving that he paid his rider scant
attention. He did ask her where she was going, and she gave
him an address on Lark Street, not far from his own apartment. They passed a casual word or two as they entered the
city, and he could have sworn later that she was there beside
him five minutes before he pulled up at the address she had
given him. But when that moment came and he turned to
look at her, she just wasn't in the car, although he had

neither stopped at any point along the way, nor could she possibly have gotten through the door which was jammed shut on her side of the car. The girl had just disappeared; if there had not been a little pool of water on the floor of the car where it had dripped from her drenched clothing, the man would have begun to doubt his senses. As it was, he sat in the car pondering what he ought to do. It was out of sheer impulse that he got out and climbed the steps of the brownstone house at the address she had given him. No sooner had he rung the bell than he foresaw what a fool he was going to appear. Just then a light turned on and the door was opened by a woman in a flannel bathrobe. He tried to figure out the look on her face but he couldn't. He was sorry to have awakened her and really, now that he had done so, he felt very awkward. But a few miles out of town he had been driving along past the Graceland Cemetery when he saw a girl in a white dress and—

"You don't need to go on, young man. I know what happened. It's my daughter again. It often happens on rainy nights; that's when she seems to want to get home. You understand, of course, that she has been buried up there for nearly four years now."

Thus I heard of Hitchhiking Hattie for the first time, nearly forty years ago, and I would be willing to wager that sometime you too have heard a similar story. For the fact is that this is the most widely told ghost story in America; it has antecedents and descendants, variants and analogues. A thousand changes are rung on it but certain elements remain constant. If we could fathom the total history of this one story, its origins, its periods of quiescence and activity, its borrowings and lendings, its mutations and constants, its sensitiveness to world events—if we understood all this about this one story we would have the answer to many of the riddles of our folk culture.

First of all, note that the hitchhiking ghost is so lifelike that it is thought by those who meet her that she is mortal. It is this misconception that gives the whole group of stories related to Hattie their point; the woman with whom a living person has conversed and had commonplace human contacts is a dead woman. Next, she is going someplace (usually home), and she accepts the generous invitation of a young man driving a passing vehicle. When her destination is reached, she disappears—or otherwise makes it evident that she is not alive. All of the stories which truly belong to this group fulfill these conditions, but there are others, bearing only a partial relationship, which also require examination.

Where does a story like this, which is to be found all over the country, get started? I don't know the answer, but we can look at the possibilities. First of all, maybe it happened. It is always told in a manner which implies that this is a true experience; the name of the city, the exact spot where the girl is picked up, the name of the street where she wanted to go, the name of the cemetery, the identification of the man as a friend of someone known to the narrator—all give it verisimilitude. As you listen and for a few moments afterward, you think, "This is a strange experience indeed"; it is only later that doubt enters in. It has the feeling of realness, and only those who have never had a vivid, uncanny experience will wish to stand up and say, beyond all question, positively and finally, "This never could nor did happen to any man." However, most of us will agree that it is unlikely that it ever happened, and most unlikely that it has happened in so many different places over the last two score of years, for the story is ubiquitous. There is every evidence that this is a folk tale and suffers the usual sea changes of its kind.

I think that in the nineteenth century there were stories in America out of which the later form developed. If it is a folk tale, where did it begin? Nor can I answer that, but I think that it has developed out of earlier Asiatic and European stories which contain the basic elements. In searching for Hattie's ancestors we might start with the Chinese. There is a book by Jon Lee called *The Golden Mountain: Chinese Tales Told in California* in which there is a story of a young man who is walking down the road one time when he meets a beautiful girl who is weeping. She tells him that she is lost and begs him to take her home; they walk along together, but as they approach the house she has indicated, she disappears. When the young man goes to the house, her father consoles him by saying that this has happened many times before and he is not to be concerned by it. Except that they walk instead of ride, this ancient version is very close to the story as told in this country.

My friend Paul DerOhannesian tells me that his parents heard it in Turkey fifty years ago from fellow Armenians. There was a young man, they say, who was traveling on horseback through a part of the country which was strange to him. He had been delayed, so it was necessary for him to ride at night. As he started to pass a cemetery he was disturbed to see a lady sitting beside the roadside, crying. He stopped his horse and asked her what her trouble might be. She told him that she had to get to a distant town, but that she was so tired and weak that she didn't have the strength to make it. He quickly assisted her onto the horse, in front of himself so that he could hold her on, and they proceeded. Galloping along he began to notice that she was continually growing heavier and increasingly difficult to hold. Never, during the entire ride, did she speak to him. He reached the town where she wanted to go about dawn, and by that time he was thoroughly frightened and worried. He dismounted and tried to help her down; it was then he discovered that he was holding a corpse. A little crowd of early risers soon collected and they were quick to put his mind at rest, or at least that's what they tried to do, when they told him that she came back in that fashion each year on the anniversary of her death. They assured him that her relatives would come along pretty soon and rebury the corpse. The girl's tendency to grow heavier as the ride goes on is similar to a trait of the Devil and of Jewish shedim who disguise themselves as sheep, or babies, or little men who grow heavier and heavier before they disappear dramatically.

In the 1890's there was a young woman—she was dead, of course—who hung around Delmar, just outside Albany, and whenever a young horseman passed a certain woodland piece on the way to a party, she would hop up behind him and not get down until he had reached his destination. From that same period and from various parts of upstate New York comes quite a different group of stories which also bear a relation to Hitchhiking Hattie of a later period. I have heard the stories from four separate localities: Hoosick Falls, Fort

Hunter, Belfort, and Milford. There is a remarkable similarity among them, as though they may have had the same kind of popularity sixty years ago as did Hattie a few years back. The rider in these stories is always a man, the driver a regular teamster, and there is invariably something queer about the rider's face. The way they tell it in Milford is characteristic:

There was a teamster who did a big business hauling freight across the back roads in Otsego County. "He was a tremendous fellow, afraid of neither man, beast, nor Devil; night nor day, it made no difference to him. One dark rainy night he was hauling freight down the line, when out of the darkness a man climbed onto the wagon seat right beside him. Never said a word, just climbed on and sat down. The teamster looked him over to see whether or not he should kick him off; he couldn't see much because the man had his collar turned up and his cap pulled down low. The teamster didn't know just what to make of it, so they rode on a mile or two, neither of them saying a word. Then all at once the man pitched off the side of the wagon into the road. The teamster pulled up and looked for the fellow, but it was so tarnation dark he couldn't see nothin'! He yelled for a lantern at a farmhouse up the road, and he and the farmer searched for the stranger, but he had disappeared; there wasn't a trace of him. Nobody would have thought much about it, but a couple of trips later they found the teamster himself lying in the road with a broken neck. He had fallen off the wagon at the exact spot where he claimed the man had disappeared into the darkness." That's the way Mr. James Rowe told the story, and while he was hardly the man to believe in ghosts, he allowed that that's what the neighborhood agreed had been riding on the wagon with the teamster, and that is what was thought in the other communities where similar events are retold. Often the rider's face is hard to see, or it is muffled. The one who rode with Clarence Hoffman, up in Belfort, climbed on the wagon near a cemetery and brought a clammy chill with his presence; the buffalo robe was flat on the seat where his lap ought to have been.

From this same period, the nineties, comes another story which bears resemblance to these, but with certain striking differences. In a number of these early stories one might suspect that the Devil is involved were it not for the assurances of the narrator that we are dealing here with the dead. And who knows better than he who tells the tale?

There was a chap everybody called "Red" who worked in Albany but lived in Kenwood, just south of the city. Every night as Red walked home from work he was overtaken by a man driving along in an old-fashioned buggy. Invariably they spoke to each other and went their separate ways. This happened for a long time, and then there came a night when it was raining hard, and that night the driver offered Red a ride, which he was glad to accept. Red tried to make conversation, but his host gave him no answers, keeping his face buried in the high collar of his coat. After a while, though, he did turn his face and Red was shocked at the bright green eyes which seemed to stare through him, and the skin which was the color of a dead man's.

"Do you feel sick?" Red asked.

Still the man stared at him while his face changed until it

was suffused with a pale glow, whereupon he disappeared. The horse started running faster and faster while the scared and excited Red did his best to stop him. In this he finally succeeded and got out of the buggy. The moment his foot touched the ground, the man reappeared in the seat and drove away as fast as he could go.

This is a divergence from our normal pattern of the hitch-hiking ghost, for here the driver himself has returned from the dead. We shall note other divergences as we move along through this labyrinth of narrative, but none quite like this one. These examples—and there are scores of others—of forerunners of Hattie should suffice to make it clear that she did not burst full-grown from the twentieth century, but that she had ancestors in other lands and earlier times. I am convinced that there is yet to be found a transitional story which will bridge the gap between the forerunners and the popular, widespread experience with which we are chiefly concerned.

One link between these early stories and the modern ones is to be found in the story they tell round Watertown of two men who were driving toward town one very stormy night when they saw a man standing by an intersection of the highway. They decided that the weather being what it was they'd give the old fellow a lift. He was a talkative chap, and when they asked him if they could take him home, he gave them the address and told them how to get there. Then there were a few moments of silence, and they turned to look into an empty back seat. Thinking that he might have fallen out, they turned around and went back over the road, but without result. When they went to the address he had given them, no one had ever heard of the man. They were still not satisfied and so began a search of old city directories and other pertinent records. Finally they found what they were looking for: twenty years before, the man who lived at that address had been killed at the very intersection where they had picked him up.

It is significant, perhaps, that this is the only instance I have heard in the twentieth-century versions in which the rider is a lone man and the only one in which the residents of his house could not identify the rider. I say *"lone* man" because there is a curious case reported from Rochester of an old man and old woman who got into a car near the Holy Sepulchre Cemetery and asked to be taken to the main four corners in the heart of Rochester, but who had disappeared when the driver reached that spot. Except for these two stories, our modern riders are always women. And with a few exceptions, they are young women, girls in their late teens or early twenties. The majority of exceptions concern a nun, but one inversion of the usual circumstances concerns a little old lady whom a young couple picked up by the gates of a cemetery not far from East Homer, in the Finger Lakes country. It was a wretched night, what with the wind and thunder and lightning, and she said she was grateful for the lift. Finally she leaned over the front seat and said, "If you'll stop right up the road a ways, I'll get out in front of that white house." But when, a moment later, the man stopped the car, she was not there. The young man was excited and went up to the door of the house, where a young woman answered his ring. She heard him out and then said, with an air that indicated that it had happened often before, "That was my mother; she has been dead about seven days now."

But the rider, as I say, is usually young, often very pretty. Her clothes are frequently a matter of note, for usually she is dressed as for a party, often in evening clothes and not infrequently in white. They say that by a bridge between Rome and Syracuse there used to appear quite frequently a girl in her bridal gown, a girl who was killed on that spot as she started out on her honeymoon. She gets in the car, and as soon as she is over the bridge she disappears. Once in a while the girls prove to be individualists and appear in red or plaid or even a dark dress.

This girl who wanted to cross the bridge (apparently one of the few American ghosts who had trouble crossing water) is unusual, for most of her sister spirits either are standing by the roadside or near a cemetery when they are picked up. If it is by a cemetery, it is the one in which her body is buried; if it is by the roadside, it is often the spot where she met her death by accident—in the Binghamton area this used to be at a bad curve on Route 17, between Elmira and Endicott, known as the Devil's Elbow. The weather, which is usually stormy, is described and the type of automobile— sedan (the most frequent), coupe, or even truck or bus— made clear. All this gives the listener the sense of verisimilitude which helps to account for the almost universal appeal of the story.

By and large, the behavior of these girls once they get in the car varies but little. Many of them are silent, except for the bare details of their home addresses; a few talk for a while, then lapse into silence. Sometimes the disappearance comes very soon, sometimes after a ride of several miles; others of the hitchhikers remain in the car up to the moment when the car draws to a stop. A whole group of them get out of the car and go in the house, but they present special problems and will be considered by themselves. A few of the girls, instead of being shy and demure, enjoy a good time.

The scene is the busy Albany–Schenectady road, the main artery between those two cities. There was a young chap who worked in Schenectady but lived in Albany, as many do. One evening he was driving home when he saw an attractive lass standing by the road and he offered her a ride. They chatted together, and she was a swell kid, such a swell kid that he suggested a date the next night. So it was agreed—they would meet right where they had that night, at the same hour. She told him her name and he left her at her home. The next night was like the one before, only more fun, and the young fellow knew that he was beginning to fall in love. Each night they met and played and parted at her door, until there came a night when she wasn't at the meeting place. He waited around for a while and then went to her home. When the middle-aged woman came to the door he asked if Mary were home.

"You mean my daughter Mary?" the woman asked incredulously.

"Yes, I'm Harry. I've been dating her, you know. I've brought her home here every night for nearly two weeks."

"My dear boy, my daughter Mary has been dead for ten years, and no other Mary has ever lived in this house."

Because Harry couldn't get the affair out of his mind, he cracked up and went to a hospital for the insane, a not uncommon experience for these drivers.

There is considerable variety in the climax of the Hitchhiking Hattie stories based on discovery of the simple, if
unusual, fact that the girl who has seemed so sadly real is
not alive at all, and has not been for some time. Usually,
having discovered that his guest is missing, the driver goes
to the door and learns the truth from the girl's mother. The
method by which she identifies her daughter may be by her
name, by a description of her and her clothing, which is the
same as what she wore when she died or when she was buried.
Sometimes the identification is made by an article left in the
car, a scarf or a handkerchief, for example. Sometimes the
young man identifies her by a picture which he sees in the
living room, usually on the piano.

I have two stories which do not belong to the hitchhiking
tradition, but which have in common with it this identification of the active dead by a photograph. One of these comes
from northern Italy where the events here told about occurred to a man who was said to have been living in Schenectady a decade ago. This man and a friend of his were
schoolboys when these events took place. There was a dance
at the next village and they begged a ride from a farmer who
was going in that direction with a wagon. After a few miles
the farmer took a different turn from the one they wanted,
so that they had to walk the rest of the way. Sitting on a mile-
stone at the crossroads was a young boy who called to them
and asked if they would do him a favor. After assuring himself that they were headed for his village, he asked if they
would carry a message to his parents. They agreed to do so

right after the dance; he gave them the message and the address. They had started on down the road a few feet when one of them looked back; at this open crossroads, where there was no possible hiding place, the boy they had left but a few seconds before was nowhere to be seen.

But these were young bucks on the way to a dance and they had no time to worry over mysteries. It was a good dance, and they stayed until the musicians went home. It was late but they decided that they should deliver the message as they had agreed to do. They wandered through the dark streets until they found the house they were seeking and knocked at the door. An old lady came to open it.

"Does the Matrelli family live here?"

"Yes. I am Signora Matrelli."

"We have a message from your son."

Signora Matrelli left the doorway, but in a moment or two her husband took her place. He was an angry man and began to give the boys a sharp lecture on the fundamentals of human decency and human kindness. The boys were puzzled. What had they done? They brought a message and they intended to deliver it.

"The documents which you are searching for everywhere are in the top drawer of the bureau where you have already looked, but under the paper in the bottom of the drawer."

Signore Matrelli turned on his heel and walked into the house. Shortly afterward they heard a shout and he came back to the door waving a paper.

Now he was all apologies. His wife had thought this was a cruel prank, for their son had been killed at a country crossroads six months before. But there was one thing he would like the young men to do for him. He brought out a group picture and asked if they could find the likeness of the boy who had given them the message. They didn't have the slightest difficulty doing it.

Another story involving a photograph was current in Albany during the depression of the early thirties. A woman was leaving one of the Catholic churches in Albany when she met an old friend on the steps, with whom she stopped to talk. In the course of their chat she said that for weeks she had been praying for some sort of job, but that as yet her prayers had gone unanswered. Her friend persuaded her to go back into the church with her, and as they were leaving a few minutes later, a young man came up to them and asked if either of them was seeking employment. The woman said that she wanted work as a housekeeper or as a companion, so the young man gave her the name and address of a lady who had just such an opening in her home. The next day the woman went to the address and asked if there were anyone there who needed a housekeeper and companion. The lady of the house said that she certainly did, but she was surprised to have anyone apply for the place because she had told no one of her need. The woman pointed to a picture on the wall and said, "Why, that's the young man who came up to me as I came out of church yesterday morning and gave me your name and address."

"My dear woman, that is hardly possible. That is a picture of my son who died six months ago."

These two stories, coming from widely separated sources and thirty years apart in time, bear a certain kinship to the hitchhiking pattern, without belonging to it. In both instances, besides the identification of the ghost by the picture, we have his considerateness of his family, an attitude comparable to Hattie's desire to get home to her family; we have the seemingly accidental meeting of mortal and revenant, the deception and eventual enlightenment of the former. Notice, too, that in the Italian story we have a dance, an element which, as we shall see, is a common feature of one group of the hitchhiking stories.

Since we have digressed at this point, we might as well go still further afield to consider the prophesying nun, whose appearances were on so many people's tongues in the fall of 1941. In New York State it was reported from Buffalo to the Hudson Valley. Basically it is the same story as the one they tell about Hattie, except that the nun always made a prediction about the war, frequently that it would be over in December of that year. It is noteworthy that in the towns near Kingston, the nun was thought to be Mother Cabrini, the first native American saint, of whom are told scores of miraculous tales.

I was anxious to see if just once one could find the driver of the car. My search took me down one blind alley after another; finally I accepted what I should have known when I began: folklore isn't history, it's art.

A taxi driver in uptown Kingston had a fare one day in the autumn of 1941 who was a nun. When she got into the car he was impressed by the fact that she looked very much like Mother Cabrini to whose memory he was particularly devoted. She said that she wanted to go to the Sacred Heart Orphanage and they started out. They began to talk about the war and the chance that we would enter it, a prospect which disturbed the man very much. She reassured him that the whole struggle would be over before December 8. Shortly after making this prediction she fell into silence, but he thought nothing of it until he pulled up at the orphanage and turned around to find his cab empty.

I have heard thirteen versions of this story of the nun who prophesies and disappears, and it seems to bear a significant relationship to another story which was current at the same time, one which concerns a prophecy but no ghostly disappearance (of these I have nearly an equal number). They told, for example, of a man and his wife who were driving down on Long Island when they gave an old man a ride. Like everyone else, they talked about the war and when it would be over. With great confidence the stranger said that it would be over in September, 1942. The couple was somewhat incredulous and took no pains to hide the fact. "It is as true," he said, "as that there will be a dead man in this car before you reach home." Shortly after that, he asked them to stop and let him out. They drove along for a while until they came to a crowd in the road where there had been an accident. The State Police asked them to carry a man who had been hurt to the hospital and they willingly agreed. But on the way to the hospital the man who had been in the accident died.

From a literary point of view the best of the stories of mysterious riders are the ones which come to their close by the girl's grave, where there is indisputable proof of her recent journeyings forth. Let me offer you two versions, each of which, with its relatively minor differences, represents a variation in the ways the people like to retell it.

There were two fellows who were driving a two-door sedan toward Schenectady. As they started to pass St. Patrick's Cemetery they saw a young woman in a white evening gown standing in the middle of the road. She signaled to the men, and when they stopped for her she asked if they would take her to her home in Schenectady. The men were in the front seat, and she sat in the rear by herself. She was cold sitting back there alone, so one of the men took off his coat and she put it around her. When they got to the address, she asked them, as a great favor, to wait a few moments till she went in the house—she would only be a moment. Then, as if it were an afterthought, she said laughing, "If I haven't come out in an hour, you'd better come in and get me." As she turned to go, she tossed a gossamer evening scarf to one of the boys. Just why they waited for her, they never knew but they did.

After a spell of sitting they both began to be restless and annoyed—as men will who have to wait for a woman—long before the hour was up. Finally the man who was missing his coat went up and rang the doorbell. When an elderly lady answered it, he asked if he could speak to the young woman who had entered the house an hour before. There had been no one entering the house that evening, and no young woman lived there. It was then that the man noticed the picture over the fireplace. "There she is, that's the girl who came in here with my overcoat a little while ago."

"But that couldn't be possible. That is my daughter who has been dead these many years."

It was then that he showed her the scarf, and she had tc

admit that it was identical to one which had been her daughter's favorite. Puzzled and dissatisfied, he went back to the car. They did their errand in town and started home. As they passed St. Patrick's Cemetery they slowed down.

"Stop the car. I want to look at something."

He got out and walked inside the fence. On a little rise near the roadway was a small, neat gravestone. What had attracted his attention was his overcoat, draped over the front of the monument.

By this time you have probably had all you want of this girl who cannot stay put once she has been buried, but who must forever be getting strange men to take her home. One more and we shall have finished with her. This is the version told by a member of New York City's police department and the scene is Brooklyn. Many isolated strands which we have seen scattered through the other versions are all brought together into the fabric of this one, which is my favorite.

Patrolman Anderson lived in Brooklyn, but his beat was up in Harlem. One night as he was on his way home in the subway, he looked across the aisle and saw a fellow staring at him. He stared right back. Finally he asked the man, "Don't I know you?"

"I don't know. My name is Jack Larson."

"Sure it is. I thought I knew you. I haven't seen you for a long time. Where've you been?"

"Well, I've been away. As a matter of fact, I only just got out of the hospital. Some people think I lost my mind. Me, I'm not so sure."

At this, Anderson moved over beside him and listened as the train hustled along the tracks.

"I had a friend who worked on the docks with me. One night we stopped in at a gin mill to have a drink before going home. There was a cute-looking girl sitting at the bar, so we went over and began talking to her. Then we bought her a drink and had one ourselves. I guess maybe we even bought a couple of drinks. When we were ready to leave we asked her if we could take her home—I had an old wreck of a car I was driving then. She said, all right, she was ready to go. But when I told her to get her wraps, she said she didn't have any. We went outside and it was cold, so I slipped off a heavy sweater I was wearing and told her to put it on. I asked for her address and she gave it to me, but when we were still a number of blocks from her house, she said she wanted to get out. I told her she didn't want to get out by no old cemetery and that I would gladly take her home and just leave her there. But she said she'd walk the rest of the way; she didn't want her folks to know that she'd been at a gin mill and picked up a couple of fellows. She was stubborn about it, so we let it go at that and drove off by ourselves.

"But she had gone off with my sweater. I didn't think much about it, but a few days later my friend and I decided that we'd like to see her again. There was something about that girl a man couldn't forget. We didn't see her around the joint where we had picked her up, so we went around to the address she had given us and asked the old lady who came to the door if Alice was there—she'd told us her name was Alice. She said there wasn't any girl lived there by that name now. Well, we told her how we met Alice and about the sweater and about how we brought her home—or almost home—that other night.

"She listened to us for a few minutes and then said to come inside. 'You wait here a minute.' She went off and came back with a picture. She showed us a picture of Alice and we said that was the girl. There was a long silence then and we started to leave. Then she said very slowly, 'That girl is dead. She is my own daughter. If you see her again, you let me know.'

"The two of us went home, but the thing preyed on our minds. A few days later this friend of mine I've been telling you about was working with me on the barge and he started to cross the plank we used as a gangplank. He got in the middle of the thing and he began to choke; he put his hands up to his throat as though someone were strangling him, and when he did it he lost his balance and fell into the water, between the barge and the dock. So far as we could tell, he never came up. Not even once.

"By this time I was getting more and more nervous. I decided to go see a doctor. He told me to go away for a while. I did, but that didn't help any; all these strange things were on my mind all the time. I got worse instead of better. I was sure I would be next. All the time I was afraid I was going to die. The doc, he said I had to prove to myself the girl was really dead, because if she was really dead, she couldn't hurt me. He said, if she was in her grave and if I was sure of it, I wouldn't worry any more. That seemed reasonable, because if she was in her grave she couldn't be in no gin mill or any other place. So the doc and I went to see the mother, but she wouldn't agree to having the girl's body dug up; nobody was going to touch her girl's grave. After we left her, the doc, he kept saying how it was necessary that I be sure in my own mind that she was buried, or I would lose my mind.

"We went out to the cemetery, the two of us, and we talked to the head gravedigger, and after we slipped him some money, he said O.K., but he didn't like it. It might get him into a heap of trouble. That night we went out there. We found Alice's grave and began work. It was tough going because it was winter and there was snow. It was awful cold and the ground was terrible hard. About halfway down, the gravedigger lit out, said he didn't think he ought to be there. We got down to the rough box, and doc was bushed and said he'd leave me to finish it up alone. I'd be all right, wouldn't I?

"I was all right. The moon was bright and I could see what I was doing. I pried the top off with a crowbar and then lifted the lid off the coffin itself. Alice was in the box all right —or what was left of her. But she was wearing my sweater."

Why do these girls wander along our highways, waiting for the driver who will stop? They are lonely, wet, unhappy; they want to go home to the warmth and protection of their mothers. But they don't quite get there; instead they go back to the grave. But they return—next week or next year—to embarrass or sadden the living. They are not yet at rest. Beside the road filled with high-powered cars, overhead the jets flying, they stand patiently waiting in the rain.

I used to have a neighbor highly trained in the teachings of Dr. Freud. He explained to me once why this story survives and thrives in an unbelieving age. I listened quite politely, then we had a drink and talked of other things. I prefer to leave its popularity a mystery, as I prefer to leave many things mysteries. I'm not one of the "old believers" Robert Frost speaks of, but on the other hand, I have tried to avoid any taint of the scientific. It's getting harder and harder to do. Good night, Hattie.

NOTES AND SOURCES

The bibliography of ghost lore and especially of ghost lore in America is not very extensive, nowhere near as extensive as the bibliography of witchcraft, for example. There is no American book so comprehensive as T. F. Thiselton Dyer's *The Ghost World* (London and Philadelphia, 1893), with the possible exception of William Oliver Stevens's *Unbidden Guests: A Book of Real Ghosts* (New York, 1945), which I am happy to recommend.

There are a few collections of American ghost tales which the hauntophile ought to have on his shelf:

John Bennett,*The Doctor to the Dead: Grotesque Legends and Folk Tales of Old Charleston* (New York, 1946);

Carl Carmer, *The Screaming Ghost and Other Stories* (New York, 1956), a retelling of a score of tales by upstate New York's master raconteur;

Jeanne de Lavigne, *Ghost Stories of Old New Orleans* (New York, 1946);

Hector Lee, *The Three Nephites* (Albuquerque, N. M., 1949), a scholarly study of Mormon ghost stories;

Marion Lowndes, *Ghosts that Still Walk: Real Ghosts of America* (New York, 1941);

Danton Walker, *Spooks Deluxe* (New York, 1956), a collection of stories told by sophisticated friends of the author;

Henry Yelvington, *Ghost-Lore* (San Antonio, Texas, 1936), a Texas collection.

Some of the stories told in this volume appeared in different versions in my juvenile, *Spooks of the Valley* (Boston, Houghton Mifflin, 1947).

In general, these stories were collected by students at New

185

York State College for Teachers, Albany, between 1940 and 1946. In the following sections the names of the collector and his informant will appear unless a source is given in the main text.

Preface from an Old Hang Yard

The folklore of Cooperstown is best found in the following books by James Fenimore Cooper (the Younger): *The Legends and Traditions of a Northern County* (Cooperstown, 1920) and *Reminiscences of Mid-Victorian Cooperstown and Sketch of William Cooper* (Cooperstown, 1936).

CHAPTER 1: *Introducing the Dead*

The story of Ferris, the lively corpse, was told to Helen Kloss of Albany by her mother. The tale of the man who milked the cow was overheard on a bus by Peggy Palmatier on April 20, 1946; Mrs. Walter J. Drew, who told Nevalyn C. Bruce about the woman who appeared in church at the time of her suicide, is a nurse and student of genealogy in Schenectady. Stephen H. Sidebotham heard of the procession of headless ghosts from Mr. and Mrs. Nathan Cottrell of Groveside; the story of the old German with his rifle full of charms was told to Doris Little by Mrs. Mary Redington, an elderly citizen of Otego. Albert Schaff, once sheriff of Lewis County, gave Genevieve Smithling the account of the headless milker, and Jane Ruth Cothren heard of the Revolutionary soldier from Miss Cora Outhouse. The worker at the Watervliet arsenal was Charles Beidle, who told his story to Janet Gould. Steve Sidebotham heard of the bloody hands from the Cottrell family mentioned above. Mrs. John O'Brien of Herkimer heard about the talking hair from the woman who heard it talk, and Mrs. O'Brien told Shirley Wurz (now Dean Wurz). Ruth Layne collected the story of the disconnected ghost from John Parker, a barber in Poughkeepsie. My filing system seems to have broken down so that my sources for the Quaker lady from Troy are incomplete—sorry. The Death Coach material came from a number of students: Ruth Donovan, who collected from Mrs. May Gagnon of a French-Canadian family in Cohoes and from Mrs. Frank Gero, Cohoes millworker; Herbert Ford from Mrs. John J. Quinn; Mrs. Ruth G. Nevin from Miss Marian Fitzpatrick, teacher in Troy High School.

CHAPTER 2: *Why They Return*

The grandfather who put on his pants was seen by Mrs. William Ten Broeck of Albany who told Catherine Martin; the murderous veteran was described to Flo Garfall of Johnstown by two neighbors, Mrs. Nina Precopia Colletta and her daughter, Mrs. Angelina Precopia Renado. The widow of Glenmont story was told by Louella Wilkes of Delmar to Eleanor Wagner. The Schoharie father who beat his daughter's suitor was a story recounted to Ruth Layne by Bill Henderson of Schoharie. The husband who sought his wife's forgiveness lived just outside Boston and the story was remembered by Mrs. E. Pettit when she talked to Marjorie Verch in Albany. The story of Mrs. McDermott, who broke up poker playing in Lowville, was also collected by Marjorie Verch, but from Daniel O'Brien, teacher and lawyer. Mrs. R. S. Jones of Ilion was raised in Walton and told her granddaughter, Peggy Palmatier, about the octagon house. The story of the priest who directed the repairs on his church was told to Louise C. Welch by her Albany neighbor, Miss Catherine Sweeney.

An Irish version of the story of the priest and mass is told by James O'Beirne in *New York Folklore Quarterly,* Vol. II, No. 3. In this version the priest is the great Father Matthew. Father Eugene Serafin, O.F.M., Croghan, told Geraldine M. Rubar about the Wellsville priest. The tale of the priest who rattled the safe comes from Mrs. James Clancy, who told Dorothy Stewart in Albany. Anecdote about the priest in Toledo, Canada, was reported to Genevieve Smithling of Lowville by her mother, Mrs. Leo Smithling. Margaret Byrne collected the story of the Visitation Parish, Brooklyn, from Joan Hylind who heard it from her paternal grandmother of Huntington, Long Island. Dennis Hannan of Glens Falls told his namesake and grandson about St. Mary's Church in that town. The lady who told Lorraine Malo of the ghostly church service in Formicola "did not wish to have her name revealed." Jewish ghost stories are very rare, if my experience is trustworthy. Abraham Shohan, from whom Rosalind V. Kemmerer collected this one of ghosts in the synagogue, was born in Smorgon, Poland, came to the United States about 1902, graduated from M.I.T., worked on the Panama Canal, ultimately became a farmer near Rhinebeck.

The story of the sailors at Sodus Bay came from Mrs. Alice Bray McGinty of Albany; Ed Strecker of East Chatham told John Witthoft about the boss of the cheese factory. The tale of old Jim, the drunk, comes from Pauline L. Petersen, who heard it from Sarah Jump of Elnora. There are a number of stories from Charles Austin of Utica in my archive, collected by Lauretta Servatius, a friend of Mrs. Austin's daughter, Edna. Mr. Austin comes from New Hampshire, is a machinist and inventor in one of the Utica mills. Three Polish stories in this chapter were told to Felicia Zielinski by her grandmother, Mrs. T. Hermus, who came here from Valno, Poland; the first of them concerns the elopers. The bridegroom who rescued his bride from the dead was collected by Herbert W. Ford from Catherine Quinn of Albany. This is one of those nubbins left from a longer, more elaborate tale, told with colorings and decorations long since worn away. For a Scottish relative which has kept its full detail, go look up "Tam Lin" (number 35) in Professor Francis James Child's *English & Scottish Popular Ballads.* The St. Agnes' School ghost story comes from Catherine Sweeney, who told it to Louise C. Welch. Lorna Kunz of Westmoreland heard about Mr. De-Vinney from her mother, Mrs. Walter Kunz.

The story of the miserly parents of East Schodack came to Mrs. Ruth Geiser Nevin from Miss Ella Bedell, R.F.D., Troy. The tale of the sinful father and his reckless son was told to Constance

T. Titterington by Isabel Malby of Albany. Mrs. Sue de Peyster reported on the mother who directed her daughter to the right bedroom. The Polish story of the road-walking mother came from Felicia Zielinski, whose grandmother told it. Michael Welch, once Postmaster of Mechanicville, but born in Waterford, Ireland, told his granddaughter, Frances Welch, the story credited to him. The story of the Pole buried on his left side is from Mary Straub, who heard it from her mother, Mrs. Joseph Straub, who lives in Chester, where Polish citizens have developed one of the onion-growing centers of the country. Katherine Egord Jackson learned about the goose woman from her mother-in-law, Mrs. Vera Jackson, who came to this country from Pruzhany as a young girl, now lives in Queens Village, Long Island.

James Casey of Schenectady told his wife about the widower and his wife's shoes; he had heard it in Dublin, Eire, from a Mrs. Garrity, who told it to a friend of Mr. Casey's on the eve of the friend's second marriage. Mrs. Madeline Cote heard of the solicitous mother from a Rensselaer beauty-shop operator named Janice.

For more about Pang Yang, see Warren Sherwood's *History of the Town of Lloyd* (New Paltz, N.Y., 1953); for more about Jemima Wilkinson, see Whitney Cross's *The Burnt-Over District* (Ithaca, 1950). See also Mr. Sherwood's book of poems, full of folklore and local color, *Poems of the Platt Binnewater*, compiled by Mabel E. L. Lent (New Paltz, N.Y., 1958).

The story of the brakeman who woke his mother was collected by Boyd R. Severn from his mother, who heard it from a practical nurse who cared for her; this is a Michigan story. Anne Murphy's mother, Isabel, told her about her neighbors, the Goodells, up in the Fairfield section. The tale of the hunters of Nyack was remembered by Leo Heymann of Congers, who told Shirley Gross. Shirley Hartz's family have lived in Callicoon for four generations; it was from a neighbor, Henry Ferber, that the story of the warning in the tannery came. Chuck Tolley himself told Richard Dimock, toolmaker and scoutmaster of Ilion, about the phantom brakeman; Mr. Dimock told Claire Crump who reported it. The Polish lady of the manor is another story told by Mrs. Hermus to Felicia Zielinski.

CHAPTER 3: *Haunted Houses*

The nailed door is a story told Louise Welch by Henry Austin. Harold W. Thompson published the story of the Hardenberg Mansion in *Body, Boots and Britches* (Philadelphia, 1940), the great New York State folklore compendium; it was also collected by my student, Ruth Fasoldt. Huldah H. Wendt says the Alder Creek story was general knowledge when she was a girl in that area. The tale of the furniture-moving ghost in Waterford was remembered by Mrs. Brouillette, an elderly lady of French-Canadian birth, long a resident of Waterford. A friend of Mary Studebaker, Mr. Wodin of Crescent, learned of the ghost there from his cousin who lived in the haunted house (Mr. W. wouldn't ordinarily have believed in ghosts but his cousin was a very reliable fellow). It was Mary Ann Ditto's family that lived in the house in Port Byron soon after they arrived from Italy; she told Ruth Blake. Shirley Wurz heard of the Port Leyden ghost from Mrs. John O'Brien. There are literally scores of stories of ghostly lights; these have been chosen at random. Thelma Gertrude Barlow's people have lived in and around Schenectady for generations; her story of hidden money comes from her mother. The dismal tale from Waterford was told to Harold Weber, Jr., by his mother.

"Four Months in a Haunted House" appeared in the November, 1934, *Harper's Magazine,* but the author had described his experience to me before the article was published. *The New York Times* carried an extended daily account of the Herrmanns' difficulties; an excellent summary with pictures was in *Life,* March 10, 1958, entitled "House of Flying Objects."

When Jane Heath worked in the American Locomotive Works in Schenectady she heard about the girls and the piano player from Mary Mele, who had heard it from her mother. The story of the blood spot was collected by Huldah Wendt from Mrs. Henry Powell. Mr. Herman Schreiber, who gave his granddaughter, Dorothea Silvernail, the charm for getting rid of ha'nts, was born near Leipzig, Germany; he came to this country about 1888 and settled near Boston Corners, New York. Patricia Dunning heard about the wailing baby from her friend, Beth Harper, whose grandfather had heard the cries as he passed the lonely chimney.

The tale of the widow of Sag Harbor comes to us from Lois Holstein, whose college friend, Eloise Worth, is a Sag Harbor native. The story of the happy crowd at Shelter Island was recalled by Mrs. Alfred Renshaw and told to Jean Adams in Newtonville. The story of the mother and child under the porch was told to Lorraine DeSeve by Lillian Carroll, an Albany secretary who summers in Vermont. Joan Quinn heard of the tale of the money behind the paintings from Mrs. P. McCormick of Troy. Barbara Updyke and Grace Shults, collecting as a team, got the story of the house where the murder was re-enacted from Mrs. Irene Lockwood of Warnerville, who heard the story from her mother and father.

I have three versions of the house that wasn't there, all very similar, all located in the Albany–Troy area: I have used the version written out for me by Sunna Cooper, who did not take the folklore course but knew I was interested. Lorraine Malo has a version about an inn outside Albany, told to her by Julia Genovesi, a college student of Italian background. And out in Painted Post, Paul Penrose heard the tale from Clyde K. Cook, but in that version it concerned a back road near Troy.

During the war many of my students married, and some of them, in doing their folklore field work, learned a good deal about their new parents-in-law and the traditions which were theirs. Jane Weir Damino was one of these girls, and it was from her father-in-law, Horace Damino, born in Castiglione, Italy, that the account of his mother came. Another family tradition came from Vincenzo Rossomondo, told to Fannie Verdiani of Syracuse. And the story of the coffin full of gold was told by Peter Marchetta to Jane Heath.

Mrs. James Huntington first told me about Elizabeth Phelps, but I have also heard the tale since from the good doctor himself. There is a charming book by Dr. James Lincoln Huntington, with photographs by Samuel Chamberlain, called *Forty Acres* (New York, 1949).

CHAPTER 4: *Violence and Sudden Death*

Louis Neubauer first reminded me of the Cherry Hill ghost; for an account of the murder, see *Trial of Jesse Strang for the Murder of John Whipple* (Albany, 1827). For the story of the Woman in White, see *West Bank of the Hudson River: Albany to Tappan* (Coxsackie, N.Y., 1906). Clarice Weeks, who was weaned on the local history of Greene County, found Sam Frisbee, retired guide, in Athens, New York.

The story of the spirit in the water came from Mrs. Rose Malerba, Albany, who told it to Frances M. D'Antonino. Dorothea Silvernail heard about Red Halloran's car from a Millerton schoolboy, Richard Miller, who had heard it in New York City. Both Paul Penrose and Isabel Campbell collected the story of the two hunters from Henry A. Austin of St. Regis Falls. Miss Campbell's version spots the scene as near Jennings Mountain between Saranac and Tupper Lake. That repulsive liver story came from Florence Garfall—who was something of a character herself fifteen years ago—and she heard it from Mrs. Grace Velardi of Johnstown, who was born in Copasela, near Naples, Italy.

According to Doris Shultes, Gordon Peattie of Beacon can take you to the tree where the Hughsonville ghost watches. For fact and fancy about Captain Kidd, see Willard Hallam Bonner's *Pirate Laureate: The Life and Legends of Captain Kidd* (New Brunswick, N.J., 1947). The G O D charm was collected by Allen Simmons from Miss Kathryn Slader of Jug City, near LeRoy; this treasure, by the way, was also protected by a man ten feet high—treasure's still there. There's a lot of Tory gold up in the Helderbergs near Berne, where Frank Hochstrasser, owner of White Sulphur Springs Park, told Ed Tompkins the charm for finding treasure. The Italian story of the little boy and the tattered fisherman was collected by Jane Heath from Mary Mele, whose mother was born in Italy and told it to her. "Mazzo Maoriello" came from James Quini, now of Amsterdam, New York—born in Supino, in the province of Frosinone, Italy—who told the story to his daughter, Victoria. The Trenton, New Jersey, ghost story was told to Margaret Seiffert by Mrs. S. N. Hanna, whose mother knew the woman who found the money.

The Pine Plains rope story was collected by Lulu Kisselbrack from Horace Bowman, whose family history has long been intertwined with the doings of Pine Plains. One of the farmers attending the Katsbaan church told the story to the summer pastor, Reverend Donald Swarthout, who told Jane Waldbillig. The story from Saugerties about the attic with no lights is from Eileen Pierce, collected from Mary Emerick, who heard it from her grandmother, Mrs. Shultz of High Woods. Mrs. Edna Leona Jones Smith collected the story of the telephone-dialing spook from her sister, Katherine J. Kinney of Ilion. The fishing ghost of the Kuyahoora Valley was part of the local tradition when Henry W. Wicks was growing up in those parts.

I first learned of the Pink House of Wellsville from a 1939 Master's thesis at New York State College for Teachers by Margaret T. Flanagan, *History and Folklore of Allegany County,* written under the direction of Professor Harold W. Thompson. Then, my student Theodora Hoornbeck collected the story from Helena Higgins in nearby Hornell. The final story is from Professor Thompson's Folklore Archive at Cornell, collected by Mrs. Edward W. Wilson of Ithaca, who heard it from Mr. Ceil Osbeck of Wellsville.

CHAPTER 5:   *Haunted History*

The Indian chief of Conesus Lake was a favorite story of George Sackett, storekeeper of that area, who told Harold Ashworth, not to mention hundreds of other summer customers. The Indian Lake story was collected by Edith and Helen Caldwell from Mrs. John S. Fish of Morrisonville, formerly a teacher at Indian Lake, whose husband descended from Chief Sabeal. "All the kids know the story of Hootin' Boys Hollow," according to Jean Hansen, who was a high-school sophomore fifteen years ago when she told it to Fred Beyer. Mrs. Ann Hamilton of Painted Post was ninety-three when she told Lucille Crants about the horse that appeared to her when she was nine. Lois Hampel Kramer was lucky enough to collect from Percy M. Van Epps, historian of Schenectady County, who told her about the "last of the Mohawks." Nick Wolsey and his revenge is taken from an excellent Master's thesis written at New York State College for Teachers by Charles F. Wilde, *Ghost Legends of the Hudson Valley* (Albany, 1937).

The Frenchmen's duel at Fort Niagara was a story collected by Jeannette Buyck from Mrs. Leslie Moore of Henrietta. My college roommate and gentle friend, Reverend Wheaton P. Webb, sometime chronicler of the country about Worcester (New York, of course), tells me he heard of Hansel of Warnerville from Grandma Mary Thurber. The ghosts of Fort Ontario were described by W. J. Coad in the Oswego *Palladium-Times,* February 28, 1941. The Fort Johnson material comes from Marguerite D. Bostwick, who learned about the Wilson family and its experience there from Miss Annie E. Wilson, who was nearly a hundred years old and in the Home for Elderly Women in Amsterdam, New York. The hoax at Fort Johnson is reported by Jeptha R. Simms in *History of Schoharie County and Border Wars of New York* (Albany, 1845).

The Horseman of Leeds deserves a careful bibliographical study which space does not permit here. So far as I know the earliest published account was in *Harper's New Monthly Magazine,* Vol. LXVII, June to November, 1883; the next year it appeared in Beer's *History of Greene County,* and later in C. M. Skinner's delightful pioneering folklore collection, *Myths and Legends of Our Land,* Vol. I, No. 25, in Harold W. Thompson's *Body, Boots and Britches* (Philadelphia, 1940), and in Charles F. Wilde's *Ghost Legends of the Hudson Valley.* Louis C. Jones, in *Spooks of the Valley,* and scores of other writers of the Hudson Valley have told it, and the people continue to repeat it, adding their own favorite details. I have used a composite version made by Clarice Weeks who grew up with the story in her ears. Sometime I hope to do a scholarly study of the relationship of historic fact to folklore in this case.

The tale of Asher Warner of Sodus Point was remembered by Mrs. Millie Pitcher of Sodus Point, the somewhat eccentric friend of Shirley Mills. Three students collected valiantly in the Lindenwald area, round about Kinderhook. Elizabeth B. Colyer fruitfully interviewed Archie LeBrecht of Valatie, and Evelyn Patchin learned from John B. Pruyn, lawyer and businessman, stories about Lindenwald he had heard as a boy from Negro servants. Word that Aaron Burr visits the orchard came from D. Pindar Jones, reported by Howard G. Bogart.

Anita Mae Leone heard about Dr. Guthrie from a schoolmate, Janet Inglehart, who heard it from the family recently living in Dr. G.'s house. For a biographical sketch of Samuel Guthrie, M.D., see *Cyclopedia of American Medical Biography* by Howard A. Kelly (Philadelphia, 1912), Vol. I. Quite a fellow. Stories about ghosts along the Erie Canal came to Shirley Wurz from her uncle, James O'Brien, himself once a driver on the canal. The item about the murdered cook was told to Howard G. Bogart by George K. Foote, that of the murder victim in the wheelbarrow, to Mary Stengel by Elmer Hensel.

Edgar Tompkins learned of Simmons's slaves from Jesse Wood, leading senior citizen of Berne. Catherine Smith's uncle, Paul

Smith, an Oneonta lawyer, told her of the Emmons station on the Underground Railroad and its tragedy.

Everybody in Salem has his own version of the Gray Man; three students brought in reports: Mary Frances Cook, Joan Sivers, and Jeanne Arnold, now a crack reporter on the *Albany Times Union*. The Civil War ghost from New Jersey was part of a conversation that took place when Jeannette Buyck of Henrietta met Mrs. Esther Sudovsky of Texas and New York City on a train trip. Mary Raymond Shipman Andrews's *The White Satin Dress* (New York City, 1930). The tale of Lincoln's funeral train was collected by Albert G. Tyler of Millerton from John W. Burgen of New York City, a conductor on the Harlem Division of the New York Central.

I have two versions of the Captain Barton story: one from Ruth McCarthy and the one I have used, collected by Helen Walsh from her cousin, Mrs. James Monahan of Auburn. I am ashamed to say that I failed to note the name and address of the woman who told me about the seaweed.

CHAPTER 6: *The Ghostly Hitchhiker*

Those interested in the scholarly treatment of this theme will find three articles in *California Folklore Quarterly* (now *Western Folklore Quarterly*): Richard K. Beardsley and Rosalie Hankey, "The Vanishing Hitchhiker," Vol. I, No. 4, pp. 303–335; "A History of the Vanishing Hitchhiker," Vol. II, No. 1, pp. 13–26; Louis C. Jones, "Hitchhiking Ghosts of New York," Vol. III, No. 4, pp. 284–292. My archive has seventy-five versions or related stories; other versions have appeared in innumerable newspaper stories, magazine articles, and collections.

The story from Delmar was told to Catherine S. Martin of Selkirk by her mother; Mr. Rowe told the Milford version to his granddaughter, June Dixon. The story of Clarence Hoffman of Belfort comes from the mother of Geraldine Rubar, Mrs. Henry G. Rubar of Croghan. The tale of Red and his strange driver was collected by Ruth Layne from Charles Van Buren of Albany. The Watertown version comes from Muriel Hughes, who collected it from Mrs. Mary MacDonald of Watertown. The couple who rode into Rochester were described by Dorothy Joyce Hall to my student Richard C. Smith. The story of the old lady from East Homer was reported by Edith Beard, who heard it from Mrs. Carrie Henry. Flo Garfall was told about the girl who has trouble crossing the bridge between Rome and Syracuse by Janet R. Smith. Ida Occhino of Endicott had heard about the boy who met the girl on the Albany–Schenectady Road and dated her, from a friend in Schenectady several years before she took the folklore course. The Italian story of the boy who sent a message home was collected by Jessie K. M. Malheiros from Frank Smith, also of Schenectady. The anecdote about the woman in Albany who heard about the job was collected by Frances Welch from Agnes Sullivan. The Mother Cabrini story told here was told to me by William Tucker of Kingston, and he heard it from his brother, Frank. This version of the dead man in the car is one of three brought in by Elizabeth Prouty, who heard it at a party in Elizabethtown. Elizabeth Dorman heard about the overcoat on the gravestone from Armida De Tommasi, at that time a clerk in the Watervliet arsenal and, finally, the story of the Brooklyn sweater girl was collected by Harriett Abrams from a New York City patrolman, Arthur Gustavson.

Many of those who told these stories between 1940 and 1946 must now be dead, and many of the girls who collected them have changed their names and moved away. I regret that I have been unable to take cognizance of these changes, but to each of the informants, living or dead, to each of the collectors, male or female, single or double, my warmest thanks.

Index

NOTE: All place names are New York State unless otherwise noted.